MW00353466

The Leading Man

Brian McGuire

Copyright © 2021 Brian McGuire

All rights reserved. No part of this book may be reproduced or transmitted in any form or by any means, electronic or mechanical, including photocopying, recording or by any information storage and retrieval system without permission in writing from the publisher.

Slainte Publishing—Irvine, CA
ISBN: 978-0-578-34436-2
Title: *The Leading Man*
Author: Brian McGuire
Digital distribution | 2021
Paperback | 2021

This is a work of fiction. The characters, names, incidents, places, and dialogue are products of the author's imagination, and are not to be construed as real.

The Leading Man
Brian McGuire

Dedication

To my immediate family for helping me with patience, tolerance and ultimately encouragement in learning that dreams can come true in writing this book.

To my parents who demonstrated the strength and discipline by coming through the depression era and WWII without acting as though they had behaved heroically or out of the the ordinary efforts in confronting difficult tasks. This quiet determination is a constant reminder of how we should all approach challenges in our lives. A special note to my father and his service in WWII, Semper Fi!

To the many teachers and life mentors I have been fortunate in having throughout my career, and who fueled my curiosity in a variety of subjects. I trust you all know who you are and what you have meant to me.

The staff of the Lamanda Park Public Library in Pasadena, CA who allowed a young boy to ride his Schwinn Sting Ray bike to their facility and lose himself among the rows of book cases. I especially enjoyed the Summer Reading Program that encouraged us to move our trains around the tracks.

...as well as the Michael J. Fox foundation for helping raise awareness of Parkinson's Disease and its cure.

Chapter 1
Why Do Good People Do Bad Things?

He felt the crispness of a New England morning as he stepped out of his room at the Birchwood Inn in Temple, NH. The contrast between the morning air and the hot coffee helped stimulate his senses for a meeting he was not looking forward to, and he pondered the "role" he was being asked to play that day.

A friend lived down the road in Rindge, New Hampshire and was not expecting a visit from Miles and would not be happy to see him, and the unannounced visit could only mean one thing for Eric Gibson...the team was on to him.

Good people do bad things for a variety of reasons...love, money and outright desperation to name a few. The difference between good people doing bad things and bad people doing bad things is they know and accept their deeds as being damaging to others either individually or as a group, and there are consequences to these deeds...a reckoning of sorts. Miles Fender, both he and Eric's names had been assigned when they had been plucked from their previous law enforcement or military roles, and they often wondered if the person assigned to establishing their new identities may have been a fan of Guitar Hero.

He hopped into his rental, a current model Chevrolet Impala, for a moment he flashed back on his grandmother's 1958 version of the same car, it was a beautiful vehicle, the first year it was manufactured, and a true collector's item in today's market for vintage cars, much the same way Miles' talents had grown. Miles knew he need to fight back the memories from his youth in Gainesville, FL. He had a role to play this morning and needed to be 100% focused on the mission. He had volunteered for it, it seemed wrong for anyone else to confront his "reckoning." These thoughts on his own past, what "roles" led him to this crisp New Hampshire morning, and what did it cost him on a personal level.

Miles had not brought a weapon to the upcoming meeting, which was completely against the policy of the team, but he knew it would not come to that. Eric would have access to his weapon, but Miles knew he could not use it against his friend, they had been through too much together.

Eric didn't expect many guests to his remote cabin in the Monadnock region of New Hampshire. It was intentional when he had it built, and only a small number of friends, both male and female, knew it existed. The surveillance team had assured Miles that Eric would be alone this morning. Eric had once been an absolute lady's man. His athletic build and ruggedly handsome face, even for a man in his mid-forties, combined with his flair for more fashionable attire, was right out of central casting for a man doing his line of work...he had been asked to play a different variety of roles than Miles, but they both had been led to this final meeting.

When Eric saw the Impala pull into the gravel filled driveway/private road, he immediately placed his Glock under the Pendleton shirt he was wearing...it was a force of habit that neither Miles or Eric could shed, and likely one of the reasons they were still alive. As Miles parked the car and unwound his 6'2" frame from the vehicle, Eric smiled, it was almost always good to see an old friend, this morning would be one of the exceptions. Eric tried to act casual in his greeting.

Eric greeted Miles with, "I'll be damned, I wasn't expecting you to walk up to my door this Morning."

Miles responded, "Well, I trust you weren't expecting someone else?

Eric still seeming glad to see an old friend, "Can I pour you a cup of Joe?"

Miles in a more serious tone, "No thanks, I cannot stay long. I think you know why I'm here and I don't want to make this too awkward."

The "awkward" reference made it sound less serious than it truly was.

The next few minutes reminded him of a passage from the classic western novel, Lonesome Dove. In it, a friend from their past has stolen a horse. In the era of Texas Rangers of that period there was only one ending for the horse thief. They knew it as well as the injured party or local law enforcement, they would be hanged. There

2

was no pleading for mercy, the punishment was set before the crimes was ever committed.

Eric asked Miles, "Do you know all the details?"

To which Miles replied, "Just enough to warrant a trip to see an old friend."

Eric somberly, "Then I won't bore you with the details."

Miles in an almost surgical reference to the matter at hand, "Please don't. I'm told you acted alone from you end, and your *clients*, an international export firm, is having their facility raided as we speak."

The transaction will have caused minimal damage to the US security, and the actual result felt as though it had been authorized as a clandestine operation to identify foreign agents operating in our sphere of influence. The problem was both Eric and Miles knew that hadn't been the case.

Eric reached back for his Glock and slowly laid it on the railing, and Miles responded with a set of handcuffs. Eric suggested, "I guess there's only one thing left to do?"

Miles pursed his lips together anticipating a final gesture on the part of Eric. Once again, he had played the scene out dozens of times in his mind, it was not the traditional way most of the leading men or women would have played it, but Miles was different, and it was one of the things, just one, that made him so valuable to the US security system. His uncanny sense of how to read people, especially the bad ones.

Eric picked up his weapon and fired a single shot. The noise echoed throughout the small canyon the cabin had been nestled in, and the noise evaporated a few moments later. Miles picked up his phone and signaled for the clean-up crew to head in. A small obit would suggest Eric Gibson died of natural causes at his vacation home outside Rindge, New Hampshire...all other Post Office, utilities, etc. would be notified. There would be no notification to next of kin. They had all been sacrificed when Eric had accepted his role. His immediate family had been notified 12+ years ago that he had been KIA protecting his country in a poorly planned war...you always need an exit strategy, and there would be no additional services.

Next Miles texted his boss, "It's done." Miles climbed back into his car. He slowly began to untangle what had led him here this morn. He was good at what he did. Realistically he was operating on "borrowed time. The life expectancy of people in his "line of work was 8-12 years, depending on the assignments and your ability to execute. He was at the outer limits of that range. He was done. He still had a chance to have a life. Maybe get to know some people on a personal level. Maybe even fall in love. He had been in love before, but it could not had happened during the has 12 years...it would have compromised his mission, any mission.

His mind wandered and he dreamed of his next role.

Chapter 2
The Next Role – Ghost's

While his boss was not altogether pleased with Miles's decision, his original "contract" had mandated 10 years of service. He had been exemplary in the quality and results achieved and had given them an extra 2 years. He had no regrets in walking away on top and was thoroughly enjoying casting himself in his last and final role.

Where would he like to begin his "retirement?" Barcelona. He had been there on 'business' a couple of times. Spain's so-called 'neutrality' in so many ways was an ideal spot for certain intelligence operations. The average Spaniard, or in this case Catalonian, cared more for the beautiful woman in the sundress standing at the cafe or the timing of his afternoon siesta, than they did world affairs, and that fit Miles just find.

The city itself had hosted many international events, including an Olympics, World Cup and had some of the most unique and amazing architecture. The centerpiece was a cathedral, the Sagrada Familia, which stands out as the most unique, the basilica has been worked on beginning in 1882 and was scheduled to be finished in 2026. The primary architect was the renowned Antoni Gaudi who passed away in 1926.

Of course, it required another Identity change. He was now Jake O'Brien, an acknowledgement to his Gaelic roots in real life, and he was a retired venture capitalist. He had done well, but not too well, and whenever questioned about his good fortune he responded with the statement... "It was hard not to do pretty well in the California tech industry." His boutique, regional firm in Redwood City, CA... Shamrock Holdings had been sold to a much larger firm and afforded him to choose whatever life he wanted to lead, within reason.

As he looked up from his paper and the wonderful and strong Spanish coffee that needed a splash of leche, he was still working on his Spanish, he noticed a beautiful señorita in a sundress...don't you love it when a plan came together, he smiled and wondered if she liked afternoon siestas? So far, Miles, er Jake had been on several "dates." They had all been lovely, including two that led to physical intimacy. While that part of a relationship was very important to him, and he loved the way many modern women from this region approached sex. They enjoyed it as much if not more than he did. This must have always been the case, but then he was a younger man it seemed as though a partner was not as likely to admit or demonstrate it. He liked the current world in this regard better and was able to catch the attention of the sundress.

Suddenly something unusual happened, his cellphone vibrated. He picked up his Android, he hated to go along with everyone else on the I-phone craze, at the same time trying to continue his gaze with the sundress. He didn't recognize the number, and there were very few who had this number. He had another local phone for his personal use in Spain. He answered, "Hola."

The other end of the said, "Kevin." The shocking thing this was his original given, Kevin Flaherty.

"Uh, no one here by that name," Jake replied.

The nervous woman's voice followed with "Oh, I'm sorry...Miles?"

He was about to respond strike two but realized what were the odds of someone knowing both these names. He wanted to simply hang-up but sensed a coincidence like this would not go away. He responded, "There's no Miles here, can I help you?"

She responded, "Miles is a good friend of my ex-husband Sam Grant. Sam always told me if I need any help I should call Miles and gave me this number. I definitely need some help now."

Of course, Jake was well familiar with Sam, a former partner in tough field operations with the FBI, they had both saved one another in the direst of circumstances, and had created a motto between themselves "No retreat, no surrender," a reference to the Springsteen song and their para-military background, he responded, "Your husband's name is familiar to me, when did you get divorced?"

The voice responded, "We're not divorced. I'm widowed and before Sam passed, he told me to get in touch with Miles."

Jake reeled with the staggering news, but still was not comfortable in playing his hand quite yet. "I'm so sorry to hear that, I'd heard he was a good man."

Leslie in a solemn tone, "Thank you. He said the same about Miles, and I really need his help right now. If you run across Miles, will you let him know Leslie Grant really needs to hear from him. I am staying at the Cotton Factory in Barcelona. Sam told me Miles had relocated here."

OMG, Jake thought to himself, this was going to make it more difficult to ignore. She was in town. The widow of a good friend who needed his help, he needed to say no, but knew he could not.

Jake spoke in a matter-of-fact manner, "Leslie, I think I might be able to contact Miles. Let us plan on the two of you meeting at the Banker's Bar in the Mandarin/Oriental Hotel at 7 PM, Ok?"

Leslie gushed, "Great, I hear Banker's Bar there has the best martinis. I could use one. Tell Miles I'll be wearing a jade-colored sundress."

Jake followed up with another question, "Will do... one last thing, you had originally asked for Kevin. Where did that name come from?

Leslie apologized, "Oh, I'm sorry. Sam showed me a picture of Miles. It reminded me of a guy I had a major crush on in high school, Kevin Flaherty. Just a funny coincidence...couldn't be the same guy."

Jake, er Miles, er Kevin's draw dropped. It must be Leslie Richardson on the other end of the phone. He had had the same feelings for her in high school, and somewhere in his parent's attic there a yearbook Leslie had signed with the following note. "I'm sorry we never got to get together. I always thought you were one of the good guys. Good luck with football. I hope we see one another someday. Love, Leslie." Was it possible her wish could come true 25 years later. He would find out at 7 PM. "Oh, what a funny story, I'll tell Miles about it."

Chapter 3
Old Habits Die Hard or You Can Get Hurt

A s soon as he ended the call his mind was flooded with thoughts, and sure enough the sundress was gone. Just as well, there would be no time for any romance now, although his memory of Leslie Richardson did conjure up some pleasant thoughts, but he dismissed them immediately...this was not going to be a typical high school reunion, unless you attended high school in Langley.

A mass of questions followed, but only several were key now:
1. Who killed Sam Grant? Why?
2. How did he have the presence of mind to send Leslie to him?
3. What is the current level of threat to Leslie and Jake?

And finally, was Leslie in the game herself to some degree? Could she be working for someone else...a bad guy? Was she even Leslie Richardson? Bad information or unsuspecting coincidences got you killed in his line of work. Wait a minute was not he retired? So much for the new role and he was just beginning to like it.

Chapter 4
Background/ Do Not Ask Questions You Already Know the Answer Too

His next call was to a friend at the FBI, Roosevelt Lincoln. He called thru the general number in DC and had his call transferred to the office in Austin. While no calls to an agency like the FBI were untraceable, this process lent itself to avoidance, he needed to be as anonymous and stealthy as possible to friend and foe alike...at least until he knew more.

Rosie could have been an NFL player, but a severely torn ACL ended that dream, and he became an internal resource for the most clandestine of operations. Too bad his playing days had not come a bit later, it now seemed they could repair anything if you were willing to do the rehab, but football's loss was the FBI's gain, and Rosie was one of the sharpest people he had ever met. For relaxation, Rosie would find the most complex 1,000-piece puzzle and put it together without looking at the picture on the cover or doing the sides/corners first...Miles could not even imagine doing it.

The call was being transferred. "Lincoln here."

Miles responded, "Rosie, this is Miles Fender." He did not disclose his new identity.

Rosie in a more familiar tone, "Well, if it isn't the old Guitar Hero. How ya been? Hey, I thought you were retired?"

Miles got right to business, "I was, I mean I am... Rosie, I heard Sam Grant passed away?" He intentionally used "passed away" instead of killed, it was always better to pretend not to know all the details, people were likely to tell you more if they thought you did not have all the answers, and while he considered Rosie a friend, in this business...there it is again, remember Miles you are retired, and you never know. It was not that he did not trust people, it is just he enjoyed staying alive more.

Rosie responded with empathy, "Yeah, very sad, are you OK?"

Miles, a bit off-guard, "Yeah, why do you ask?"

Rosie, "The folks that got Sam are looking for you. Good thing you already got disappeared."

Miles trying to catch-up, "Wait a minute are you saying Sam was killed, executed?" He also wondered why no one from the agency had alerted him. Did they think his new cover was that airtight?

Rosie continued," Yep, serious stuff. They told him they were not only going to kill him, but everyone he loved in this world. We just heard his parents were killed in a horrible traffic accident and his only sibling was mysteriously killed in a zip line accident near Glacier Park in Idaho...it appears the line was intentionally cut, so far that is all we got. I'm glad he and I weren't closer...sorry, bad joke."

The attempt at humor was ignored by Miles, Rosie, was Sam married?" Again, better to act less informed to get more and hopefully corroborating information. Sometimes the intelligence game felt like a massive game of Post Office. Stories get changed, either accidentally or on purpose, it was always best to be begin with a tabula rosa, those Latin courses really paid off, and develop your own set of facts.

Rosie responded, "Yes, absolutely. Leslie was/is a wonderful woman...smart, fun, and easy on the eyes."

Miles interjected, "Rosie, you slipped and said, *was*. Is she on the list?"

Rosie continued, "Not yet or not that we know of...she flat out disappeared right before Sam was killed. We figured Sam had a premonition on what was about to go down."

Jake, er Miles thought...or someone else tipped her off. You never know, and as he recently reminded himself, you be careful, or you may get hurt.

Miles now asked, "Rosie, something you said earlier suggested I might be connected in some way?"

Rosie announced, "Sorry buddy, but you're as big a target as Sam was. We've determined you and Sam had bounties of $1 million and Leslie is/was $2 million!"

Jake felt a shudder throughout his entire body, it had to be the cartel, those guys had lots of money and long memories. He went on to say, "Well, that's very flattering in an odd sort of way, but why is Leslie's higher than Sam and mine?"

Rosie sensing some lighthearted probing, "Are you jealous? Honestly, we are not sure. We have two theories, killing her would have hurt Sam immensely...and you know better than anyone how cruel those mofo's can be."

Jake rubbed his face with his hands. "Yeah, don't remind me." Some bad memories came swirling back in his mind, including the most difficult decision he had ever made. "You said there were two theories?"

Rosie in a more official tone, "Yeah, we're thinking Leslie may have been working for someone else."

Miles persisted, "Like who, good or bad?"

Rosie followed with, "We're thinking good, doubtful Sam could have been compromised by anyone else."

In a strong affirmation Miles accepted this conclusion, "I agree, Sam was one of the best, I miss him already." Jake thought for a second about who or what Leslie was connected to. There were even more clandestine units working under the FBI or CIA, and he had also heard rumors about privately funded vigilante groups who hated organizations like the cartel and did not feel the legitimate law enforcement agencies were doing a good enough job or were hampered by their own laws and regulations. He had even been approached by one prior to his "retirement," but he thought he was done.

Rosie's next question triggered his instincts to takeover, "Hey buddy, where you hanging these days? Maybe you should come in for a formal briefing?"

Jake responded, "I'm in Florence." The fewer people who knew his actual whereabouts the better. Even a friend like Rosie...the next comment hit his antenna hard, along with the little hairs on the back of his neck.

Rosie asked another question he should not have, "Hey, I heard about Eric, tough deal for you?"

There were only three people living or dead that should have known about his last assignment...Jake, his boss and Eric. This type of a breach in protocol, especially with a member of an internal team, was never communicated outside the acting parties...there was never a need to know otherwise, and Eric had technically committed suicide.

Jake said flatly, but with an edge to his voice, "Not sure I know what you mean."

Rosie retreated, "Oh, I get it. Sorry I brought it up. Let me know if you need anything else?"

Jake finished with, "I will, thanks for your help."

Jake had another issue to be concerned with now. They were beginning to pile up. How had Rosie heard about Eric? It could be a random break in inter-agency protocol or worse. He had filed it away for another day. He felt as though he was punching the proverbial time clock again.

Chapter 5
Back in the Game

Jake was back in work mode. He was never truly off it, but certain things, like checking for tails were coming back into his SOP...standard operating procedure. He needed some time to process what he had learned and needed to get some rest. His intuition told him it could be a busy evening or few days.

He swung by his condo. He loved the quiet luxury of his 3-bedroom unit with a view of the Mediterranean. Barcelona was a medieval city that had embraced the 21st century. It had been nearly destroyed during the Spanish Civil war, a full-blown rehearsal for WWII, and Francisco Franco never liked this center of Catalonia. Catalonia reminded Jake of Texas in a certain way. They thought of themselves as Texans first and Americans second. Nothing disloyal or unpatriotic, they just loved their home state more. The same observation could be made of Barcelona and the region it was in.

Jake grabbed an overnight bag. He decided to get a room at the Mandarin/Oriental Hotel. His plan was not fully prepared, nor would it be, but he thought access to a room may come in handy later. He laid down for a 30-minute power nap, it was no longer a siesta, waking from a siesta occasionally had something positive to look forward to...a glass of sangria or occasionally a warm body that was fully rested and looking forward to a great start to the late afternoon or early evening, such would not be the case today.

As he dozed his mind drifted...

Chapter 6
What Could Have Been

rowing up in Gainesville, Florida Kevin had thought of himself as Robert Redford was described in the film, The Way We Were. His character it was said to had "things came easy to him." In many ways Kevin had lived and idyllic life. His parents Jim, an accomplished professor of Engineering at the University of Florida, and his mother, Elizabeth a "stay-at-home mom" who had been anything but just a stay-at-home mom. She was involved in every stage of Jake's life, a little league coach, not a team mom, and an advocate for learning, not in the way some mothers were strict about homework, but in the way of describing the world in such an amazing style that you just had to learn more about it. She had also been an Olympic volleyball player. This dedication to both learning and athletics made Jake the well-rounded person he had become through his first 18 years.

The Gainesville High School District was "open," meaning a student could file to attend any of the six schools. Buckholz was considered the ultra-academic and sports school, with Eastside struggling to gain status as a magnet-type program, even before the term was commonly used. Eastside was racially balanced and would require a bus ride to attend. Kevin talked to his parents and decided he wanted to help create something special, rather than join something that was already special. Oh, and Eastside had something else that would become "special," and incoming first-year student named Leslie Richardson.

Kevin was a realist from an early age, especially when assessing his own skills. He was an exceptional athlete in all sports but decided to limit his activities to just football and baseball. This was done so he could pursue his other interests on a more academic basis, student government and music, plus girls.

Football was his first love, his sophomore year he made varsity and by his junior year he was playing both ways, QB and Strong

Safety, and as a senior he was all state as a defensive player. He was being recruited heavily by the Gators at University of Florida, and even though he had other elite schools after him, he wanted to stay close to home and help the local team. He knew college would be the end of his sports career, he was a great high school athlete, and would be good enough to play in college, but was sure his skills would top out there. It was OK, he had plenty of other things he wanted to do.

Then came that fateful day in June, a notice from the Selective Service, he was being drafted. His soon to be coaches assured him they had ways to get him out of the draft. Their lawyers could fix anything. Jake's buddies from Eastside did not have those options and it bothered him...what made him so special? Later that day he came home and told his parents he had enlisted in the Marine Corps. They both cried and then his mother hugged him and told him how proud she was of him.

Vietnam was an unpopular war to say the least. Kevin moved quickly up the ranks and was given command of a platoon in the 1st Marine Reconnaissance Division, an elite unit that worked behind enemy lines. Later he was asked to develop a select team to be involved in recovering downed pilots in North Vietnam. They were exceptionally good at this rescue operation and rescued dozens of downed pilots. Kevin reckoned that if you asked pilots to fly these missions you needed to promise them 'someone would come and get them'.

Unfortunately, Kevin's chopper was ambushed in their final mission, the downed pilot was used as bait to draw in the more important target. Kevin deployed to get the injured pilot when they touched down. The pilot had been moved into chopper, and as Kevin made attempted to climb aboard the chopper he was hit twice by enemy fire. The chopper pilot made a difficult decision that Kevin was gone and lifted off to spare the rest of the crew. The NVA pulled his dog-tags and sent them through channels confirming he was KIA.

Kevin was awarded the Medal of Honor posthumously. His family and friends had a small memorial for him that was attended by several Marine and Navy pilots his team had saved. His parents never fully recovered. His mother took it the hardest, and in the end

15

their marriage suffered the final casualty of Kevin's service to his country.

Kevin was not dead. His wounds were not as severe as believed at the time. He recovered and was sent to a POW/labor camp in Laos. A year and half later, and after being subjected to many atrocities at the hands of his captors, the camp was "liberated" by an elite group of commandos intended for this type of clandestine activity. One of them recognized who Kevin was, and while convalescing at a US Naval Hospital in Tokyo he was briefed on his family's demise. This news made it easier to accept his recruitment and the role that had led him to Barcelona...and now this predicament.

He dozed fitfully and headed over to the hotel.

Chapter 7
Old Habits Die Hard

Jake arrived at the bar 30 minutes before they were to meet. He needed to "case the joint" and find a good spot to observe Leslie's arrival. It felt like old times...unfortunately.

At 7 PM she entered wearing the aforementioned jade sundress. She was even more striking today as a woman in her early forties, then she was as an 18-year-old high school senior. Some people have good genes, others must work at it, and some had both. He suspected Leslie did both.

He decided to treat Leslie as an amateur. His suspicions had grown since his call with Rosie, but he decided it would be an easier adjustment is he started with her being a non-professional.

She ordered her martini and glanced around the room. She did not see him, nor did she notice the man who had followed her in. It would be nice to presume he was just another guy who saw a beautiful woman in a jade sundress and thought he had a chance. This was not the case, there were several telltale signs that gave him away...the way he scanned the room, the newspaper prop he carried and the way he watched her and the room.

He dialed her number and after she said hello, he replied... "It's Miles, don't look up, take this as a call from a friend, now say it's great to hear from you." She repeated as instructed. "Ok, listen carefully you've been followed, I want you to finish your martini and pay the bill in a casual manner. Once you are finished go to the elevator and take it to the 12th floor. As soon as you get off the elevator go to the stairs up to the 13th floor. Go to room 1327, the door is ajar. Go in and lock it behind you. I will meet you there. When I knock ask for a password, the password is Stratocaster. If the person does not know the password call security. Do you understand?"

A nervous woman who was clearly not expecting this behavior replied, "Yes."

Jake left the bar just as Leslie motioned for the check. He had already chosen a spot where she could not see him, and he could wait for the tail. Go time!

As instructed, she paid the tab and headed towards the elevator. She may have been nervous but did not show it. She boarded the elevator and pushed 12, after getting off on 12 she immediately went up the stairs and found room 1327. The door was ajar, she went in and locked the door behind her.

Moments later the tail arrived at the 12th floor. He strolled down the hall looking for a sign of where his target had gone. Jake was coming the opposite way. He had "borrowed" a name tag from one of the hotel's managers jackets. He wanted to blend in and look official. In his best rudimentary Spanish, he inquired "Puedo ayudarlo senor- Can I help you sir?" The tail responded with a gruff "no." Jake then asked him," Eres un invitado registrado - Are you a registered guest?" The tail responded "si - yes." Jake being persistent and wanting to create an opportunity to eliminate the tail from his role, asked "Puedo ver la llave de tu habitacion - May I see your room key?" The tail, now clearly frustrated with the line of questioning began turning to confront the overzealous manager and was surprised to have his jaw hit squarely by the fake manager's fist.

The tail knew immediately this was not coming from a hotel manager and Jake who had delivered previous knockout punches was shocked the tail remained upright. What ensued was more of a scuffle than he had anticipated. Jake prevailed but had taken some hits. His nose was bloodied and one of his cheeks had been cut. He dragged the unconscious man into the stairwell and stumbled up the stairs to 1327, He passed the code on to and Leslie opened the door.

She gushed, "Oh my god your hurt!" he responded with a line every guy wished he could use "Yeah, you should see the other guy." As she held the door open, he went back into the hallway and pressed the fire alarm. He explained to her that is how he wanted the trash, meaning the trail, to be disposed of and help to cover whatever their next steps would be.

Chapter 8
Vamanos (We go.)

They say one of the most powerful instincts for the animal world, including humans, is the impulse of "fight or flight." Jake understood this impulse better than most, but in the world he recently attempted to retire from, there was typically more data to draw from. He knew when an operation was going bad, the options to correct whatever the problem was, the ability to assess whether it needed to be aborted and where the "safe house" or other means of extraction were...and most importantly, who he could trust. None of these options were completely available to him and he would need to improvise, with a few exceptions.

Leslie looked hard at Jake... "It's you, isn't it?"

Jake replied sternly "There's no time for a reunion now, quick change into this" he tossed her a shopping bag with a different colored sundress, a straw hat, sunglasses, and sandals.

Leslie looked puzzled. Jake barked "They'll be looking for a jade sundress, this may buy us a few seconds and that could make a difference for us." Leslie immediately pulled the jade sundress off, exposing an athletic figure that she clearly worked at and was not to shy or embarrassed to reveal. Jake had turned to try and respect her modesty, but Leslie had acted on his directions so quickly he almost had to steal a glimpse.

As Leslie completed her changing, Jake shared their next steps... "We do not know if your friend was acting alone, so we need to get out of here right now. It is imperative for the next few minutes for you to do exactly what I say. Understood?" Leslie nodded her head. She had a frightened look, anyone with any coherent thoughts would, but Jake sensed a level of confidence as well. Jake liked confident women.

They left the temporary safety of the hotel room and boarded an elevator. Jake pushed the button for floor 2...he nodded at Leslie and said simply "We cannot leave through the main lobby." After getting off on the second floor, they took the stairwell down to an emergency exit. The alarm had created some cover and Jake had pre-arranged to have his car, a European version of the Audi A6 with several refinements, merely 50 meters from the exit. They entered the car and Jake pulled away from the confusion he had intentionally created, Step One was successful.

After several minutes of silence Jake broke the ice... "Yes, it's me. I am not sure how or why this coincidence occurred, but we can sort this out later. I have several questions I need answers to right now, OK? Leslie nodded her head yes. "Do you have a cell phone?" Again, a positive nod. "Can I see it?" She handed it to him. Jake quickly opened the back of the phone, examined it, tore it in half and through it out the window. "There was a GPS transmitter, someone wanted to know where you were. We'll get you a new phone."

Jake went on... "Who knows you were here and what your plans were?"

Leslie thought for a moment... "Just a friend of Sam's from the FBI that he told me I could confide in... kind of a guardian angel for me."

Jake asked quickly, "What is his name?"

Leslie responded, "He's a really great guy, Roosevelt Lincoln."

Jake asked, "when did you tell him you were coming here to find me?"

To which Leslie responded. "A few days ago."

Jake prodded her, "Don't use words like 'few', I need you to try and be as precise as possible, was it two or three days ago?"

Leslie said "Three, I'm certain of it."

Jake picked up his phone and dialed the only person in the US security system he could trust, and who as well had the authority to get things done.

A surprised voice of a friend muttered "Miles?

Miles responded, "Yep, it's me.

The friend questioning, "I thought you retired?"

Miles, "Me too. I need your help."

The friend, "OK, shoot."

Miles in an almost mechanical yet efficient manner, "I think we have a rogue FBI agent. I need you to investigate his behavior quickly, and at the very least shut him down temporarily, got it?

The friend responded, "Sure, what's his name?

Miles, "Roosevelt Lincoln."

The friend, "OK, I'm on it!"

Leslie had an incredulous look on her face. Jake responded, "I spoke to Rosie yesterday. He asked me where I was. People in my business, especially friends don't ask questions they know the answer to."

Leslie blushed. "But."

To which Jake responded, "If I'm wrong, I'll apologize, if I'm right, it may buy us some needed time, either way I'm OK with it."

Jake followed up, "Now who else knows?"

Leslie looked a bit perplexed.

Jake pressed, "It's not that hard of a question."

To which Leslie muttered "Well, Hector."

Jake in a direct mode, "Who's Hector?"

Les casually, "A friend."

Jake persisted, "What kind of a friend, a lover?"

Les bristled, "I don't like that word."

Jake in a serious tone, "Well, I don't like lots of words, especially the ones that can get me killed. I am not here to judge you, I have only one goal...to keep us alive. Now who's Hector?"

Leslie stammered, "You have to understand, Sam traveled a lot, sometimes for months at a time. I..."

Jake interrupted, "Listen, I don't really care about the why's and any regrets you have, I just need the cold hard facts...how long had you known Hector, how did you meet him and how long were you being intimate?"

Leslie appreciated his bluntness and the use of the word "intimate" ... "It was about, er...6 months, I met him at the club, we had a drink and he offered to give me private tennis lessons and one thing sort of led to another."

Jake asked, "Were you going to leave Sam?"

Leslie gasped, "Of course not, it was just fun and filled up the time I was alone."

Did Hector ever suggest you should leave Sam?'

Leslie mused, "Not that I recall. Why do you ask that question?"

Jake replied rather clinically, "If a man, of relatively modest means, is having a romantic relationship with a woman of means, it usually follows that they may want that person all to themselves.

21

Again, I am not judging, just need all the data to develop our next steps."

Leslie nodded and thoughtfully and with the romanticism of her relationship with Hector beginning to ebb, "Do you think Hector fits into this?"

Jake again in a clinical tone, "If I had to guess, Hector is either dead or working for them."

Leslie was beginning to process the exchange of information more easily... "Who are 'them'?

Jake ignored her last inquiry, "Any others?"

Les with raised eyebrows, "Lovers?"

Jake persisted, "No, others who knew you knew you were coming here to meet me?"

Leslie smiled, "Oh, no."

Jake smiled to himself, he often thought if he wore the right collar, people would be quick to confess to him. He turned to Leslie... "Now do you have any questions?"

Chapter 9
A Safe House

It was almost 8:30 PM when Jake and Les had reached the car, about 90 minutes (about 1 and a half hours) of pure adrenaline rush and discovery between the two of them. Jake had initially thought of heading towards a friend, someone he knew he could trust in Valencia, but it was a four-hour drive, and no one was happy to have a guest, friend or not, show up after midnight.

He also realized he had not been "made" by the "bad guys" ...at least he didn't think so, and his condo could serve as a safe house, at least for tonight. He adjusted his route and turned to Leslie.

Jake opened with, "Your turn."

Leslie started slow, "Oh, yeah...where are we going?'

Jake responded, "Somewhere safe"

A leery Leslie, "Is that all you can tell me?"

An adamant Jake, "It's all you need to know...and sometimes the less someone knows the better."

An even more leery Les, "Don't you trust me?"

Jake stern and honest response, "I don't distrust you, but trust needs to be earned."

Moving on Les asked, "OK, who killed Sam?"

Jake reacted, "Whoa, starting with the heavy stuff. Well, unfortunately, in our line of work we make enemies. Usually they cannot locate us, or do not have the means to retaliate. Again, and unfortunately, Sam was in a more visible position that was more likely to draw attention. We talked about it, and I warned him about it, but Sam thought the good guys needed to be visible. Good people needed to know good people were looking out for them. He was an inspiration to me on what it felt like to be a good guy."

Les followed up, "You didn't answer my question."

Jake assuredly, "100% the Cartel. We hit them pretty hard, and they have the means and attitude to act out their revenge."

A now concerned Les, "Did I lead them to Sam, thru Hector?"

Jake mused, "Probably not...but you led them to me."

This embarrassed Les, "Sorry, I didn't...I didn't know, er understand."

Jake corrected her, "How could you. Plus, this might be better for me than a random hit out of nowhere. At least I... we have a fighting chance."

Les looking less certain, "You think so?"

Jake feeling confident, "Oh, I know so."

Chapter 10
An Introduction / Nice to Meet You!

After a peaceful night in Jake's condominium the two awoke refreshed, but with clearly a great many concerns on what to do next. However, Jake already knew what his next step would be, he needed the help of a good friend...someone he could trust.

Jake assured Les there would be time soon to "refresh her wardrobe." Going by her hotel was not even open for discussion. Instead, they climbed in the Audi and began a drive towards Valencia. It was 3 1/2 hours of the most beautiful ocean, or in this case sea, scenery you could ever imagine. During it Jake took all the precautions necessary to avoid any unwanted company. there were several sure-fire tactics for a driver to avoid "tails."

The drive also gave the two of them a chance to talk...Les began with, "You must think I'm a horrible person?"

Jake trying to seem understanding, "Why would you say that?"

Les, blushing, "Oh, you know...Hector and all that."

Jake confessed, "Les, I've seen and done things that would make your head spin. Besides, I decided a long time ago not to judge others. I'll leave that to a higher pay grade."

A somewhat relieved Les, "Well, thank you, I guess...it's not critical for our mission, right? By the way, it sounds like you're a religious man."

In an almost absent-minded manner, "I have faith...you know what they say, there are no atheists in a fox hole. Hey, you used 'mission' in the last sentence, that sounds like operator jargon. What would you describe as our mission?"

Les, "I read a lot of spy books. I'd say our current mission is to stay alive."

Jake agreed, "I'm all for it. Phase 2 will be to get those responsible for Sam's death, including those unpatriotic bastards who may have sold him out."

Her time to agree, "I won't disagree, but it seems we're a bit out gunned right now."

Jake in a more amusing tone, "No problem. A good agent, and I am a particularly good agent, will pick them off one at a time. By the end, the remaining survivors will be climbing the walls knowing they are next. Watching them squirm is half the fun?

In a bemused tone, she was beginning to like this guy, "Fun! You really think of it as fun? It sounds like torture to me.

Jake barked, "Les, you have to understand the agent's mindset. There are good guys and bad guys in this world, and we know which team we are on. Sometimes you need to cross the line, but it always seemed justified to me. They're killing Sam just made it a little easier for me to "cross that line with malice."

A now curious Les, "What will my role be in all of this ...?"

Jake opined, "Hopefully very little, I think. We may use you as "bait." initially, but after that you will be taken to the local embassy and 'disappeared' the way I did until yesterday."

A truly apologetic Les, "Kevin, I mean Jake...I'm so sorry about that."

Jake trying to let her off the hook, "We've been all through that and it could not have been avoided. Once I heard about Sam I would have reactivated anyway. Can't let the bad guys get the upper hand."

Les changing the mood, "OK, but changing the subject...do you remember me from high school?"

Jake smiled as he said, "Of course I do. You were out of my league, but I always had hope that I could earn your attention. You were the lead actor, and I had a supporting role."

Looking straight forward into the horizon, "That's nice of you to say, and I felt the same way. Do you remember how I signed your yearbook?"

Jake with another smile, "Yep, you thought I was a good guy and that we might see each other again."

Les demurred, "Well I guess I'm clairvoyant as well."

A hopeful Jake, "Well, I hope you can tell me how this story ends?"

Les muttered under her breath... "I hope the guy gets the girl." and then hated herself for even thinking it.

26

Chapter 11
Old Friends

The drive to Valencia went by quickly and allowed the two of them to become reacquainted in an odd sort of way. They even managed to have a few laughs remembering people and events from high school, including their mutual interest in one another, with neither being able to "pull the trigger," a rather poor pun that had them both smiling. However, none of their lightheartedness could ever remove the seriousness of their current situation

As they pulled into a small compound outside Valencia Leslie sensed a softening in Jake's tone. The compound included a small Spanish-style hacienda with a gravel driveway and that other than an open gate was surrounded by a 10-foot wall. Whoever lived here valued their privacy.

The compound was littered with gorgeous cypress trees that our indigenous to Valencia and captured Leslie's attention. She had studied Landscape Architecture in college and loved the use of indigenous plants and trees in any landscape design. It caused her to have yet another brief yet pleasant flashback.

As Jake stepped out of the car a man about the same age came out of the house with a beautiful señorita. As he gestured and spoke quietly to the young woman, it felt to Les as though she was being dismissed, not how you would treat a spouse or girlfriend.

The man approached Jake with outstretched arms...

Daf gushed, "Well, how's my old friend, Kevin or Miles or whatever you call yourself these days."

Jake replied, "Thank for the help with my cover, Daf" ...as he nodded towards the young woman exiting the compound.

An apologetic Daf, "Oh, sorry, I thought you were retired."

A further scolding Jake, "Once again..."

Finally getting it, Daf "Oh, I get it, loose lips...sink ships"

They embraced. Jake's friend was Lieutenant Donald "Daffy" Drake, USMC ret. and who had served as Jake's, then Kevin, primary helicopter pilot. He was not on the last il-fated mission Jake had taken and had summarily decked the other pilot upon his return after leaving Kevin for dead on the battlefield. The striking of a fellow officer could have led to a court martial, but the leaders decided a LOA and return to the states was the proper "punishment."

Daffy was never quite the same after the seeming loss of his good friend, and fortunately, due to a nice inheritance from his grandfather, was able to live as an expat in Spain. He was also the only other person, until now, who knew the whole story of Miles journey, and was about to learn of his reincarnation in becoming Jake.

BY dusk they were all caught up and into their third bottle of sangria...

Daf exclaimed, "You sonofabitch, you're living 3 1/2 hours down the road and never reached out to me."

Now it was Jake's turn to be apologetic, "I was planning on it, I really was, I just needed to sort some things out."

Daf quoted, "You need to stop sorting and start living...like the line from Shawshank."

"Get busy living or get busy dying...words to live by."

Jake looked over at Les and rolled his eyes. "Do I get to play Red or Andy?"

Daf shouted "Neither you get to play Kevin! You are reconnected with the girl who should have been your high school sweetheart. This is the best do-over of all time."

Jake mumbled a line he remembered from a Hemingway novel, The Sun Also Rises... "Yes, it's pretty to think that way." He continued with "It must be nice to live in that romantic world of yours, I'm sorry I don't have the same luxury. I'm just a washed-up Marine who tried and failed to serve their country."

Daffy erupted, "FAILED!! Do not ever use that word about my friend Kevin. Do you know how many pilots were able to return to their wife and kids because of him...you."

Jake replied tersely, "That's enough."

But Daffy was not hearing any of it. "Enough? I'm just getting started. Remember, I attended your memorial in Gainesville. I saw them hand your mother the folded flag, and your father the Medal of

Honor you received posthumously. I heard the Honor Guard firing a 21-rifle salute and the playing of Taps, and...'

Jake persisted, "And what?"

A clearly emotional Daf, "And I cried like a baby."

Leslie froze, she had never heard this part of Jake's story, and had rarely, if ever heard a man speak as passionately about another man, to the same man. It was overwhelming.

Daffy continued "and then on top of all that a rescued pilot shows up and introduces his two-year-old son to your mom and Dad...they named him Kevin."

Jake could not take any more accolades, it made him extremely uncomfortable, and he uttered a poor attempt to dislodge the tone of this rehashing of his glorious past... "How about those Dolphins?"

Daffy couldn't help himself... "Dammit! Are you sure you're Irish? You're certainly not acting like it."

Chapter 12
My Angel

That night the nightmares returned for Jake...as they did to some degree most nights, but these were intensified due to the discussion from earlier in the evening. Sure he, or actually Kevin then, had been a hero to the many pilots and their families he had helped to rescue, but in the end, he had paid a horrible price for his actions. And while his country had heralded him a hero, posthumously, the VC sympathizers staffing the camp in Laos had also figured out who and what he represented, and these nightmares brought back the worst of the cruelties that had been imposed upon him during that time.

As he suffered in a semi-conscious state reliving these atrocities, he somehow felt the soft, yet strong pull of a body enveloping his own. This was not part of his subconscious, it was real, and his body initially tensed with the feel that was followed by a soft whisper of "it's going to be OK, just relax" that comforted him in a way he had never felt before. Jake exhaled mightily and fell into the comfort of Leslie's embrace.

She was only wearing one of his t-shirts and the room was completely dark. The softness of her smooth body coupled with the strength he felt in her arms and legs caused him to melt into her embrace in a way he had never experienced. He so wanted to roll-over and see what his body was feeling, but Les must have sensed this desire and simply whispered "Just close your eyes." He did as instructed, and fell into the deepest, most consuming sleep that he had ever experienced.

The next morning, he awoke, stretched, and quickly rolled over, but his vision was gone. He stumbled into the bathroom he shared with the other guest room without hearing the shower running. Before he could reverse his entry, a voice sounded that reminded him of the dream, he had just awakened from... "Can you hand me a towel?" Again, he did as requested. The shower door was steamed up so that only a silhouette of her body was visible. After accepting the towel through a small slit in the door, Les emerged with the towel fastened securely just below her shoulders and just above her knees...it was a vision Jake wished he could see for the rest of his life. She had been stunning in the jade sun dress, but this was an entirely different and more intimate look now.

Jake, still in his pineapple decorated boxers, managed to stamper out... "Thank you for last night."

To which she replied, "Your welcome, Sam had nightmares too." The mention of her deceased husband and his good friend changed the mood immediately, and as she stepped back into her own room she softly said, "You owe me one."

Jake stood and pondered what had just happened. Rewinding the tapes from the night before and thinking "No he hadn't, and yes he did."

Chapter 13
Shopping

The name Valencia is feminine for "strong/brave." How fitting Jake thought for a woman who had been able to chase away a nightmare from his deep and tortured sleep. He wondered if she could or would do it again.

As the three met up in the great room of Daf's hacienda, they enjoyed strong coffee and breakfast pastries that were delivered daily from the local panaderia, and suggested activities for the day.

Daf suggested, "Perhaps I can round up some other ex- US military friends to help?"

Leslie followed with, "A visit to the US consulate requesting protection as US citizens."

They then both turned to Jake expectantly and said in unison "What do you think?"

Jake pondered their looks and comments and muttered, "I think we should go shopping."

As Jake viewed their incredulous looks, he again smiled and looked directly at Leslie, "I told you in Barcelona after our hasty departure we'd get you some things."

Leslie protested, "I can get by with what I have..."

To which Jake responded, "No need to, I'm sure they are not on to our location yet, and even if they were they'd need to gather the resources, besides YOLO...You only live once."

Who was this new man sitting with them? It was a man who was learning how to sleep without nightmares.

Chapter 14
Just One Day

Like most European cities Valencia was a combination of medieval and modern architecture. This was indeed the case with Valencia and the contrast was stunning. Valencia was the 3rd largest city in Spain following. Madrid and Barcelona. Through the centuries it had been occupied by Spaniard's, Visigoths, Moors and Spaniard's again led by the Famous El Cid, portrayed by Charleston Heston in the 1961 blockbuster film.

Spain's neutrality in WWII had spared it from the annihilation brought forth on many other cities and towns on the continent. However, the pre-WWII Civil War in Spain had done tremendous damage to both Valencia and Barcelona.

Americans had fought, and many died, fighting against the fascists led by Franco. These memories placed them in good stead with the locals as Daffy had learned and experienced.

The Spaniard's also had a unique take on worldwide geopolitical status. They had once been a world power, as demonstrated by Cortez and his followers in removing a tremendous cache of gold from the New World. Most of this was now found in the beautiful cathedrals that dotted the Spanish landscape or squandered it in other non-glorious ways. Many traditional Spaniard's yearned for what could have been, but the younger generation felt blessed in a way...being a world power was not what it was cracked up to be or as an American teenager might say, 'overrated'.

None of this meant much to Jake or Leslie as they behaved like most young couples enjoying a wonderful afternoon in this beautiful city. They laughed, Leslie tried on clothes to replace some of what had been left behind and even strolled arm in arm at one point. They both needed a brief respite from what had been a tension filled high wire act for a few days.

Later in the afternoon they settled in a small street side cafe for a bottle of sangria and a platter of olives, cheese, and chorizo. Jake turned to Leslie and said, "I can see why Sam fell in love with you."

Leslie responded with a shake of her head and a slight blush and asked, "Why do you say that?"

Jake sat back and rubbed his hands on his napkin... "I think you'll find I say exactly what I mean. In this case, I've got a glimpse of a beautiful, confident, fun-loving young woman and... I can see how Sam fell in love with you."

Les stammered, "Well, I'm really none of those things."

Jake left the romantically tinged feelings at this point and regained the seriousness that had kept him alive until now in this deadly business... "I shouldn't have said it. It was inappropriate. You are freshly widowed, and I have lost a dear friend. The fact is I have no idea what love is or how it feels. It was a luxury I was never allowed. I am envious of the two of you and terribly sorry it had to end so abruptly. I'm sorry."

Leslie gathered herself and removed her brand-new Ray Bans... "I am too. The fact is I will never stop loving Sam. Even If I'm given the chance to love again. It would have to be someone incredibly special, and I am glad Sam put us together. I hope with all my heart you will get your chance. You deserve it!

Jake said to no one in particular, "I do too."

Chapter 15
What It Feels Like

As they rose from the table Les moved forward to hug Jake and whispered, "I wish things were different...I wish you would have asked me out in high school, I would have said yes."

This simple confession hit him like a ton of proverbial bricks. In what Bob Dylan would have described as a 'simple twist of fate' could have changed everything. He might have fallen for her, avoided enlisting, played college sports, and saved his parents' marriage/lives by asking a pretty girl out on a simple date. All he could manage following this cascade of broken dreams was... "I do too."

As they strolled back towards the compound Jake noticed the grass was greener, the sky was bluer and the soft breeze blowing through the cypress trees. Could this be what falling in love felt like?

As they entered the gates, they saw Daf talking with the woman from the day before. she was visibly sobbing and Daf motioned for the two of them to join he and the woman. Daf explained Maria was indeed a high-end escort of sorts, and when not with Daf she considered other clients. She was hurt when Daf dismissed her upon their arrival yesterday and ended up with a stranger from out-of-town.

During their 'time together' he mentioned he was being paid to locate two people who had recently traveled from Barcelona. In her haste to please her new client, payback Daf for dismissing her so hastily and undoubtedly, to secure a large tip, she mentioned Jake and Leslie to him, including where they were staying. He then bragged that his client was bringing two professional hit men with him on the 10:30 AM train from Barcelona.

Daf turned to Jake and muttered, "What do you think?"

Jake replied absently and with what seemed to be the weight of the world upon his shoulders, "Well, at least it's not High Noon," in thinking of himself and Leslie in the roles play by Gary Cooper and Grace Kelly. Oh, and so much for the feeling what it must be like to be falling in love. He was jerked back into reality mode.

Jake looked back at Daf, "Can we trust her?

Daf responded quickly, "I'd trust her with my life!"

To which Jake responded simply, "Good, because we'll have to."

Chapter 16
Transitions

For a man wondering if he was falling in love moments ago, Jake was switching back into professional mode. Leslie noticed the transformation first, and while she liked the softer Jake much more, she felt more comfortable with the business version in times like these. Just like when things got tougher for Sam on a case, the more humane version began to peel away, and a tougher, almost scary version appeared. The good news was the more humane and kinder version always returned.

Jake walked directly towards where Daf and Maria were standing and queried her, "Were you in this man's hotel room?"

Maria seemed embarrassed, and looked towards the ground like a scolded child, but replied "Yes." This confirming what everyone already knew.

Jake, with almost no emotion, "Will you take me there?"

This time Maria did not speak, but firmly nodded her head in the affirmative.

At this point Daf felt compelled to say something on her behalf, "Now Jake, I don't want to get her involved in our problems."

Jake gave Daf a sideways look and said in a monotone voice, "She got herself involved." And then added, "They're not your problems, it's just Les and me that have a problem."

Daf at first bristled at the comment and then summoned a line from his favorite movie, Tombstone... "Well Wyatt, that's a terrible thing to say," suggesting Daf would not help a devoted friend in a critical time of need.

Jake, knowing he would have reacted in the same way, and for all the roles he has played in this life, being a hypocrite was one he had tried to avoid at all costs. He was compelled to respond, "Oh, alright."

Then again in professional mode, "OK, we need to do three things 1) Maria you're going to introduce me to your new friend, 2) Daf, if this is going to be the Alamo, I need to know if there are any weapons and 3) Les, we need to talk."

Before going with Maria to meet her new friend Jake did two things, called his friend in the upper echelons of US security to check on local assets, and reviewed Daf's home armory.

The asset question was positive in a limited way, as was the armory inventory. Daf had three handguns, all workable and in good working order, and two 12-gauge, pump action shot guns with a plethora of ammunition for each...Jake could not help but ask his friend if he was worried about a zombie invasion, to which Daf responded, "You can never be too well prepared." In reviewing the ammo situation Jake offered, "If either of us has to reload, we're dead."

He sought out Les next. She was in the kitchen washing things over and over, and otherwise trying not to think about what was going to happen in the next 24 hours. Jake walked in and uttered "Les, we need to talk."

In the most cavalier of voices Les replied, "About what?"

Jake smiled, he appreciated the obligatory humor in the face of danger, "About what's going to happen in the next day or so." Les interrupted,

"Don't tell me there's nothing I can do; Sam was my husband."

Jake had expected a response along these lines, but admitted it sounded different coming out of her mouth. He went on, "There are things you can do, and there are things you can do, but never should or want to, and there are things you should flat out never do. Regardless, what is going to happen tomorrow will change a person's life forever. As someone I care about, I really don't want to expose you to it."

Les only could muster, "Then why do you and Daf need to see or do it?"

Jake could only respond with, "Because we've already been there, and listen...if anything happened to you after what's happened the last couple of days, I'm not sure I could live with myself."

A teary eyed Les replied, "Well maybe I feel the same way."

Chapter 17
In Harm's Way

After assuring Les she would have a role to play in tomorrow's proceeding that would keep her out of 'harm's way', as well as assuring her his plan would be safe for him as well, he gathered Maria for the first phase of his plan.

The Hotel Palacio was a stately old hotel near the Nord train station. After some brief surveillance of the lobby bar and restaurant, Maria walked Jake to the room where she and the stranger had spent the last evening together. As planned, Maria knocked on the door. A voice from within spoke in Spanish, "Quien es -Who is it?" In Spanish. To which she replied, "Maria."

This was her cue to head down the hall, her job complete. The stranger opened the door with a smile on his face like he was expecting a redo of the night before. Instead of Maria's loving embrace, all the stranger saw was the muzzle of Jake's Glock followed by a short punch that broke his nose, knocked him down and left him semi-conscious on the floor.

Jake quickly bound and gagged the man in a secure fashion. He then located the man's phone and scrolled to his text messaging log. As he had hoped, the man had been communicating with his boss via texts...Jake now had control of where the battle would be fought tomorrow.

As expected, there was another knock on the door. Jake opened it and saw two men in overalls, the local assets as promised, "We're here to pick up the trash." Jake examined the man's passport to make sure he was not someone else and allowed the assets to complete their roles. The man would be interrogated later that evening, with any useful information forwarded to Jake. Step 1 complete

Chapter 18
A Plan

As Jake made his way back to the compound, he continued to work through the plan he was conceiving. He knew that if he could compromise their communications and choose the site for the upcoming battle, there was a good chance he would prevail...even against a much stronger foe. They would be confident in their numbers, always a dangerous attitude in any type of a fight, and the element of surprise would always help 'even' the playing field, or in this case 'battlefield'.

Once back in the safety of the hacienda, Jake described to Les and Daf what would take place tomorrow morning. Les would serve as the lookout, and Jake emphasized to her its importance in the success or failure of the day's activity. While it truly was a key tole for their minimal resources, his other priority was keeping her out of harm's way. He and Daf would set the primary trap and would alert her after it was sprung.

However, there always needed to be a plan to escape for if things went bad, and all three new where the rallying point was, and what the evacuation plan would be. Jake knew that neither he nor Daf would be able to make it to the 'rallying point' in the event going badly, but he needed to make sure Les knew her way out.

Daf then helped translate the texts between the apprehended stranger and his boss. As Maria had explained previously, the main group of three or four would be arriving at 10:30 AM tomorrow by train, this was key. Beyond the simple translation Jake and Daf looked at the style of communication, use or miss use of grammar, misspelled words, slang, etc. Any changes in style could create doubt, or worse yet, cause them to make a call.

Jake and Daf then reviewed their 'arsenal' of weapons once again. Both would begin the battle with shotguns. While these may not kill their targets initially, the were most likely cause some damage and disorient them momentarily. If things went right, they would finish their respective job with handguns...there would be "No retreat. No surrender" (in Sam's honor) and no prisoners.

Once assured everyone knew their role, they enjoyed a light meal with a bit of their now favorite sangria. There would be no 'overserving' tonight, they all needed to be clear headed tomorrow. They said their Buena's Noches and headed for their respective rooms, all of them knowing there would not be much sleep-in store for them, especially Jake, who at least knew a sleepless night meant no nightmares.

Chapter 19
The Awakening

Just before Jake entered his darkened room, he felt Les slip her hand into his, she then whispered in his ear "Just in case."

A startled Jake responded and turned towards her and responded with "Just in case what?" Although he already thought he knew what she meant.

Les to his other hand in hers, looked up and kissed him softly yet firmly on the lips and whispered again, "Just in case something happens tomorrow," she paused briefly and looked away before she followed with, "I don't know how else to thank you and... I can't bear the thought of not knowing how this would feel."

She stepped back and began to unbutton the blouse they had bought together earlier in the day. After a couple buttons she stopped and looked back at Jake and said, "What are you waiting for?"

To which Jake said, "Absolutely nothing."

As it turned out, while Jake had been physically intimate with women in his past roles, he had never truly 'made love' to anyone. That night with Leslie created a whole new world for him. He had known there was something else to life and had always hope it would find him...he doubted he could find it. Leslie showed him the absolute best of it.

After which she lay next to him and again whispered, "Now get some sleep, my turn to watch over you." Jake knew there would be no nightmares.

Jake awoke the next morning with a completely different view of life. This time his vision from the previous night was still with him. His initial instincts were for an encore of the night before, but before he could act, Les slipped from under the sheets and pranced into the shared bathroom and shower, she blushed in saying, "We'll get back to that later."

With the evening and those words Jake's life would forever change. He now had something as never before to live for...the love of a good woman, and as he reflected on how wonderful it all was, he heard Les again, "Hey, can you get me a towel?" This time she was not as modest as the previous morning, but she did cover herself with the towel.

She followed Jake back into his room, as she sat next to him and surveyed the bedding is disarray, she commented, "What happened here?"

To which Jake muttered, "Everything."

With his new view of wonderful life could be he revisited the 'fight or flight' principle once again. His first thought was to grab Les and get "Out of Dodge!" To do whatever it took to be in her arms one more time. He shared these thoughts with Les, it was the most intimate conversation he had ever had with another person.

After they shared these thoughts with one another Jake shook the beautiful notion from his head and declared, "No! It ends today. I'm tired of running."

Les leaned over and with yet another soft, firm kiss said, "Me too."

Jake thought silently to himself, "Those SOBs won't know what hit them."

Chapter 20
Something to Live For

While Jake externally expressed a quiet confidence in the day ahead, it was mostly for his comrades to observe and hopefully feed from. Inwardly, he was a jumble of nerves on what could transpire. Jake had always since leaving the Marine's acted on a solo basis, with a few exceptions involving Sam Grant mostly. Nevertheless, by noon he suspected it would all be over.

Both Daf and Les new their roles and understood their absolute necessity in following of following the script exactly as written. There could be no ad-libs in today's performance, which is people in these types of events got worse, or worse yet, got killed. The thought of anything happening to either of them, especially Les, was a dark thought that he could not allow his brain to consciously consider, on a subconscious basis...it was always there.

Maria had been sent away to Seville to run an errand for Daf. There was no real 'errand' and Jake had suggested it to Daf to make sure she was not involved in today's activities. In fact, she did not know any of the details of their plan, she had already demonstrated her ability to share valuable information to the wrong people.

Unbeknownst to Les and Jake, and while they had been shopping the day before, Daf had summoned his attorney and banker. Whether it was a premonition, or just tidying up loose ends, Maria was the co-beneficiary of his estate, Jake had been named as well in the form of Kevin Flaherty. If Jake, er Kevin did not survive the entire estate would flow to Maria, with instructions to donate in Daf and Kevin's names to Wounded Warriors, it would be a fitting tribute if things went bad.

Jake had his first cup of coffee and reflected on what had transpired during the last year. In Rindge he had officiated over another friend's suicide, that in many ways set the stage for his "retirement" and led him to Barcelona. His retirement, in which he was becoming, content, but had now discovered through Les was not enough. He now wanted more, and Les was the vehicle to get him there.

Just then she walked over and leaned against him, "A penny for your thoughts?"

Jake did not respond immediately, instead he wrapped his free arm around her shoulders and mouthed the words, "Thinking about the future."

Les drew herself closer, "Am I part of it?"

Jake initially said, "I hope so" and then realizing his role in keeping things positive recanted his statement to "I know so, if it's OK with you?"

Les smiled and buried her face in his chest, the chest that last night had felt like the safest place in the world, and said, "Jake, you'll never get rid of me."

Jake pulled her closer and thought, "This is much better than being 'content'."

And then the stranger's phone buzzed...ACTION!

Chapter 21
No Dress Rehearsal

It was 8:45 AM and the two of them froze. Jake quickly alerted Daf who translated the message to a simple, "We're boarding the train now." They all collectively had a sigh of relief. This was exactly what they had hoped for and rehearsed. Their response, communicated in a manner that was consistent with the stranger's style was, "I have some good news for you when you get to Valencia." They had so wanted to probe more with questions about how many, and if they would be joined by others in Valencia but feared if they deviated from past styles of communication, it could be a red flag. It would be Les's role to be the scout.

There was a one-word text in return, "Bueno!" Again, it was just what Jake and the others had wished for and would allow them to 'bait the trap' exactly as planned.

Daf and Les wondered if they should get to their stations, and he advised to relax, the train was not even due for over an hour and a half, lets enjoy the morning. This calm attitude leading into violent action had been reinforced by of all things one of the principles in Coach John Wooden's Pyramid of Success... "Be quick, but don't hurry." This zen like approach to coaching clearly was applicable to non-basketball activities. His calmness was absolutely required at this moment

At 10:30 AM the phone buzzed again, and the text read, "Esas son buenas noticias - So what is the good news?"

As scripted, Daf texted back, "I have apprehended the two American's and their friend at a home not far from the station."

This was indeed good news, but the leader was upset that his advance scout had acted beyond the scope he was given. He shrugged this feeling off for now, noting he would council him afterwards, and reminded himself how capable the man had always been in following his commands. A subtle scolding would suffice. This was extremely good news. His leader, the new head of the cartel that had seen its operations severely wounded by Sam and in this case Miles. He smiled and thought to himself, "The success of his mission would bring him great favor within the cartel, and a large bonus.

The last thing he texted was a request for the address and little did he know the conversation he was having was with his intended targets.

The hook had been baited. As soon as Daf sent the text, Jake announced, "It's Showtime, places everyone." He gave Les one last hug and said, "It'll be fine, it will be over soon."

Les accepted his words and thought of all the things it could mean...Sam's murder would be avenged; Jake could retire once again and just maybe if everything could really work out, she could have a beautiful new life with a boy she had had a crush on in high school.

Jake had similar thoughts, but immediately went into work mode. He was reminded of a line from a Kevin Costner film Open Range. In the film his character had unwittingly fallen in love with the sister of the town doctor, as he and his friend had begun their walk to an uncertain destiny he said in his goodbye to her, "Men are going to die today, and I'm going to kill them." It was not delivered in a bragging or overly dramatic manner, just a clear statement on the seriousness of the situation. The taking of another life should always take with complete seriousness...it is not normal to say the least, and no matter what the other had done or was planning to do that was wrong did not temper what you needed to do.

Jake had tried to explain this emotion to Les the day before. Good or bad, win or lose, her life was about to be changed forever. Even as a witness and not the person personally responsible for killing someone else, it changed you. He just wanted to make sure he would be there to help her through it.

Chapter 22
Not the OK Corral

As the three moved to their assigned positions, Jake had a nagging thought that kept tugging at him. One of the last planning conditions they had all agreed on was that 'win or lose' and no matter who survived, they would need to prepare for a quick exit. Les had gather all their items, and Daf was to pack enough for a one week cooling off period. As Jake moved the Audi outside the compounds' gate, he looked in the trunk once more and was surprised to see only their gear...there was nothing packed for his friend.

Before Jake could remind Daf his phone buzzed with a text, "They're here, three of them." Jake would need to remind Daf later.

As Les scanned the street for potential intruders from her fully concealed spot her thoughts began to wander...what if things did not go as planned, could she imagine life without Sam and now Jake? She remembered a line her father had shared with her as a child, "Don't borrow trouble." In other words, do not worry about a negative outcome before it happens, it is a complete waste of energy.

These words allowed her to refocus on the matter at hand. She picked up three men headed towards the compound. They were all wearing over-sized coats to conceal their weapons. As they drew closer, she began to make out their faces, and she had a positive ID on one of them. It was Hector, she flashed back on what Jake had said three days before... "He was either dead or is with the cartel." She felt like she could either vomit or scream.

Two men she had been physically intimate with were about to face one another. One she had a ferocious hatred for, and the other she had hopes would be her lifetime companion moving forward. She had a tremendous urge to alert Jake but realized it would only distract him from what he needed to do... "Don't borrow trouble."

Jake knew this would not be a scene from the Shootout at the OK Corral. It would be over quickly if everyone played their parts correctly. "If" was a word that professional like Jake 'avoided with all his might'. It was one reason he preferred to work alone. When it was just him there were no "if's," it either happened or it did not, simple.

Jake had to be the "trigger man." He was the one who had been in these situations before and would not hesitate at the wrong time. It was Daf's role to be a brief distraction while Jake assumed his shooting position. He would come out to the front porch to a spot that was marked. He would display two open hands to the strangers with a greeting in Spanish of "Puedo ayudario - May I help you?" Daf had both cover and his shotgun within three feet. Once the strangers verbally responded, it was Jake's cue to open fire. As soon as Jake fired both loaded cartridges, Daf would do the same. After the 2nd salvo, Jake would finish the job with his Glock. Daf had a handgun of his own tucked in the back of his pants and covered by his shirt in case Jake missed or was incapacitated. Jake knew he would not miss.

The shotgun blasts would not kill a man from the distance they were being fired, but the pellets within the cartridges would sting. The shotguns were being used to disorient the intruders and buy Jake and Daf a few seconds. Time was the key ingredient here.

Daf stepped out his front and instead of the agreed upon script, uttered the words "Quien va alla - Who goes there" in Spanish, much like a sentry challenging someone on a military base. Jake knew his friend would not miss his lines that badly, there was a reason for him to ad-lib. Jake could only move as quickly as possible, without hurrying, to have a clear shot to help his friend.

Before the intruders could completely respond with, "Nosotros estamos buscando uno amigo - We're looking for a friend." Daf drew his handgun and began firing. Daf never had been an expert shooter and firing a handgun at a range of 40-50 feet was tougher than they made it appear in movies. Simultaneously, Daf bellowed, "Soy Miles Fender y tu estas en mi propidad – I am Miles Fender and you're on my property!"

This was the target they had come for and he drew their complete attention. There had been no disorientation or stinging pellets to distract the intruder, they returned fire towards Daf's position...he had not taken cover either.

Jake's brain processed this unexplained change in plans, he knew there had to be a purpose, so he sped up his actions and fired his shotgun from even further away from his designated spot.

As soon as both cartridges were expended, he dropped the shotgun, not wasting time to see the impact it had and drew out his trusty Glock. He fired three times and then there was complete silence.

Chapter 23
The Waiting/A True Friend

Les would say later it was the longest three minutes of her life between when the shooting started, and she retrieved the "clear" text. Even then she held her breath, it could be Daf sending the text and Jake was "incapacitated." God, she hated that word.

The scene she saw reminded her of the words Jake had prepped her with earlier, "There are things you never want to see." What she saw was three men lying in the middle of the driveway that approached the front door of the hacienda. They were clearly "incapacitated" and more likely dead, either Jake or Daf would have been sure to 'finish the job', if necessary.

Further ahead and near the front door she could see two men, one was tending to the other, but from this distance she could not tell whom. She took the next few steps in trepidation...

Jake had reached his friend quickly after making sure the intruders were dead. Each receiving a single bullet in their chest creating lethal damage to the heart. In concert with his examination of the wound he muttered, "What was that all about?"

Daf in a strained voice said, "Don't you get it, Miles is dead. You're free!"

Jake responded, "You idiot, we would have figured out something." He knew his friend's wound was lethal.

Daf in a more whispered tone, "Promise me you'll make the best of it." His eyes drifted for a final glance at Leslie.

Jake nodded his headed firmly in the affirmative and pulled his friend closer.

Daf mouthed the words, Semper Fi and drifted off.

After he laid his friend back down. He stood and turned to Les. She thought his expression was the most unique combination of sadness, anger, relief with a tiny hint of joy for good measure. They then literally fell into one another's arms. Les' emotions were more heavily weighted towards joy and relief, with some regret for her earlier momentary thought that she hoped it was Daf who had been wounded and not Jake.

Jake let go of Les for a moment and pulled out his phone to call the local assets he had used the night before, "I need you here stat."

Meanwhile, Les had walked over to the fallen intruders. Of course, there was only one who interested her. She stared down at him with the pure hatred she felt earlier, along with a dose of anger directed at herself for being played so easily.

Jake wandered over after ending his call and followed her gaze to the man he had just killed. "Hector?" he asked.

She nodded and reacted indifferently by shrugging her shoulders and stating, "He had it coming."

Jake nodded, he wanted to say something like "Let that be a lesson for whomever messes with my girl" but thought better of it. Technically she was not his girl yet, and he never wanted to take things for granted. He instead opted for "Please go to the car, I'll be there in two minutes."

As she turned to head to the car, she turned to survey all that she had witnessed and saw Jake standing over Daf in as complete a salute as you could imagine. These were clearly different men than she had encountered throughout her sheltered life. She knew now that Sam had been one of these men as well. Men who willingly put themselves in harm's way for a variety of reasons; good versus evil, God and country and more than anything...friendship. It was a true brotherhood.

She would miss Sam for the rest of her life but being thrust into the arms of Kevin made it different. She had something to live for and could not imagine life without it.

Chapter 24
Aftermath

Once they were in the car there was about 5 minutes of needed silence before anyone spoke. Jake had reached across the center console and was holding hands with Les, but they both needed to process what they had witnessed, especially Les.

Finally, she offered a soft lament, "You warned me."

Jake could only respond with, "About what?

Les continued with, "That there are things you never want to see."

Jake began to apologize, "I'm sorry, I should have sent you away and handled this without you having to see it firsthand."

Les in an almost scolding tone interrupted his apology with, "Absolutely not! I needed to see it. I needed closure. I..."

Stepping back in Jake retorted, "Well, I hope you find it. As you have seen from my nightmare's, closure is an elusive process for me...there are things that stay with you, always."

Les let go of Jake's hand and placed her hand on the top of his leg, slightly squeezing his inner thigh with the tips of her fingers and exhaling with, "Will you help me try?"

Jake glanced over and smiled, "With all my heart."

This brought a soft smile from Leslie with a straightforward question, "Where are we headed?"

Jake did a similar exhale and said, "Madrid, it's about 3 1/2 hours from here." It was approximately the same distance from Valencia from Barcelona. The terrain was much different than their last drive, with the absence of an ocean views the most glaring departure. Plus, Jake was almost certain they were not being followed this time.

Les followed with, "OK, I have two questions; 1) what happened back there, and 2) what do we, assuming there is a 'we' going to do now?"

Jake pressed his straightened arms against the steering wheel to stretch and relieve tension. He then started with, "Daf went off script."

Les quickly responded with, "I saw that, but why?"

Jake in an almost monotone manner said, "To give us our freedom."

The words hung there for both to fully appreciate before Jake continued, "Miles Fender is dead!" Les looked perplexed...was that not one of Jake's aliases. "That idiot had to be a hero. He knew I would never agree with such a plan...not in a million years, but in killing Miles he gave the cartel what they wanted, and we are free to 'live our lives'. I can never forgive or thank him enough."

Les took a while to let that soak in, "Do people really do that kind of thing?"

Jake again exhaled deeply, "It's amazing what the human spirit is capable of...our people back there will work with the Spanish authorities to convince everyone that an American national named Miles Fender was killed in a shootout with the vindictive members of a Mexican drug cartel. May he rest in peace."

Les with another dose of obligatory humor stated, "That's too bad, I kind of liked that guy."

Jake smiled and laughed with, "I never liked him, he was an ass."

Les cooed, "But easy on the eyes, if you like the ruggedly handsome look, which I happen to." Her hand left its resting place on his leg and squeezed his upper arm, "But I think there's plenty of other guys like that around here."

Jake, "A few..."

Les looked away absently, "What about Daf?"

Jake looking straight forward, "He will be buried with full military honors at Arlington. As he should be." He continued, "But I will never forget him and have a long-term idea of what to do in his memory."

Les squeezed his arm again...she liked it when he thought 'long term'.

Chapter 25
A Place of Many 'Dreams'

Other than the capital of Spain, Madrid is one of the greenest cities in the world and has more cloudless days than any city in Europe. It is also the highest capital city in the European Union. The name Madrid comes from the Arabic word "magerit" which means "place of many streams."

The Hyatt Regency Hesperia Madrid was a modern 5-Star hotel within a short walk to the US Embassy on Calle de Serrano. Jake asked the Concierge to make dinner reservations for 7:30 that evening and headed to their room to spend some time resting and cleaning up for dinner. Unbeknownst to Les, Jake had three "outfits" sent to the room for her to consider for their first nice dinner together. Jake thought how nice it felt to do something special for a person you cared about and have them appreciate it as much as she did. It had never happened to him before.

As she slipped out of the last option and chose their favorite, Les went over to the bed her fluffy white hotel robe. As she untied the strap in front she said in an alluring tone, "Just in case, I was wondering if we could make love before dinner?"

Jake quickly agreed and pulled a bottle of champagne from the room refrigerator and found what he felt was an appropriate music channel, the Gypsy Kings made the atmosphere exactly right for the late afternoon and early evening. Jake could not have been happier, and he thought Les seemed the same way.

The rest of the night was like a dream. The dinner, the conversation, the intimacy of sharing his hopes and dreams with a person he loved. He slept in her arms once again and the nightmares stayed away.

Chapter 26
Have a Little Faith

The Cathedral Church of Armed Forces is a 17th century Baroque-style, Roman Catholic church located in Madrid. Since 1980 it is the Military Cathedral of Spain and the seat of the Archbishop of Spain. It was declared Bien de Interes cultural in 1982.

Attending Mass had been a good call. The cathedral was magnificent, and the military theme felt appropriate as well. While the dominant language was Latin, with additional remarks in Spanish, they were able to discern what mattered most, including lighting a candle on behalf of Sam and Daf.

The embassy was a short stroll from the church and provided a few moments to reflect on what the future could bring...Les began the conversation as follows: "So much has happened to us these last few days, I think it will be good to settle down and think what we both want to do?"

Jake thought he heard some hesitancy in her comment, that Les felt their relationship had happened too quickly and in too dramatic life or death fashion, perhaps she needed to step away from him. He replied with, "I understand completely, you need to sort things out on your own, and if down the road there's something you'd like to explore between the two of us we can reconnect."

Les stopped dead in her tracks and turned to Jake. She grabbed both his hands in a manner that was reminiscent of how she had in Daf's hacienda, "No, that's not what I meant at all, you are the only certainty I have in this world. I need you...I love you more than you'll ever know!"

She hesitated for a moment and followed with a more uncertain tone, "Is what you said what you want?

Jake felt a warm glow, a tingling throughout his body. He paused and contemplated her comments just long enough for a concerned, almost frightened look develop on her face. Again, he took a long breath, exhaled, and said, "You just made me the happiest guy on the planet. I thought I needed to offer you some independence but hoped like hell you would not take it. I truly cannot imagine being without you."

It was her turn to blush and feel the same tingling feeling, "I'm glad we're on the same page and most importantly, I'd do anything for you."

Jake displayed a devilish grin, "Anything?"

She slapped his arm and said, "Well almost anything. I promise I'll be good to you" she said with a combination angelic, devilish grin of her own.

They were almost to the gate when Jake stopped, "One last thing, I'm not particularly good at this, not yet. I have never been in love before, and I am sure I will do some dumb things. Please be patient."

Les quickly added, knowing they needed to check-in at the gate to the embassy, "You're in love with me?"

Jake traded devilish grin for a serious, but heartfelt... "I fell in love with you in Valencia."

His comment was not entirely true. In many ways he had fell in love with her in high school.

Chapter 27
A Grateful Nation

They were met at the gate by Lieutenant K.D. Clark, USMC. He was dressed in his formal Marine "blues." Jake remembered feeling as though that uniform made him feel ten feet tall. It was almost impossible not to look and feel great wearing it.

Lt. Clark shook both their hands and announced he was at their service for as long as they remained in the embassy. He added, "Sir/Mam, feel free to ask me anything."

He gestured and spoke, "Sir/Mam this is to the Ambassador's Chief of Staff."

Les demurred and slipped her hand, "Doesn't he look cute? Do you have one?"

Jake responded, "Not the look he was going for, and yes, if it was buried with me in Gainesville." It had simply been placed in his coffin, along with other memorabilia.

The Chief of Staff, John Arnold met them at the door and after an official sounding introduction gestured for them to join him at his conference. He then turned and told the Lieutenant, "That will be all, I'll send for you when our guests are ready to be escorted from the embassy."

Mr. Arnold turned back to his guests and offered coffee or any other form of refreshments. They accepted and another lower ranked Marine brought in a complete tray. Mr. Arnold smiled and said, "Don't you just love Marine's? They always do the right thing for our country."

Les patted Jake on the arm and agreed with Mr. Clark, "Yes, I do." Jake smiled and nodded in acceptance.

Mr. Arnold asked if they would call him John? They again nodded and suggested he do the same thing.

John began, "The Ambassador on direct orders from Washington have advised me to extend every courtesy available. In essence, that is the most generous an embassy can extend to an American citizen. Jake whatever you and Leslie did on our behalf must have been extraordinary."

Jake nodded and silently muttered 'thank you', he was used to being thanked for activities that could not be addressed due to national security. Les was less modest, again patting his arm and exclaiming "He's a true American hero."

Jake gave her look like that's enough. She hadn't fully learned yet how Jake like to fly 'a bit under the radar'. She smiled, thinking to herself, "Well you're my hero."

John's first question was "How long do you plan on staying in Madrid."

Les spoke first with a grin, "Until we're tired of it." She looked over at Jake for confirmation and found him deep in thought.

He finally looked back to her and suggested, "How about four more days, we need to catch our breath, but I have some other matters to attend to back in the State's, is that OK sweetheart?"

Les had initially been taken aback by this 'change in plans' and then remembered there had been no original plans. Plus, this was the first time she had been addressed as 'sweetheart', she liked it and replied "Yes, honey."

John now the next matter of business are the names you will be traveling for passports, tickets, etc.?

Les again responded first, "Yes, my maiden's name Leslie Richardson."

Jake responded, "Me too."

Both John and Les looked at him puzzled by his remark.

Jake apologized, "Oh, I'm sorry. My given name, Kevin Flaherty." It was time for Jake to reprise his original role/name and see what good needs he had left.

Les smiled and looked over at John and said whimsically, "The boy I fell in love with."

John had no idea what they were alluding to buy nodded and said it shall be done. He then asked them if he could make any travel arrangements for them. Jake asked for a one-way ticket to Gainesville, Florida. John looked expectantly over to Les and she said, "Me too."

John nodded in a way that indicated it would be handled. "Now, before we move on is there anything else we can help the two of you with at this moment?"

Jake, not yet switching to Kevin asked if they could get an English version of the primary newspaper. John said it wouldn't be a problem and reminded them that lieutenant Carter would be their liaison for any additional needs.

He then asked if he could change the subject to which Jake nodded in the affirmative. "A friend of yours recently passed away, a Donald

Drake. Coincidentally he passed away in Spain and has left you with a large portion of his estate."

Jake looked over at Les and rolled his eyes in a manner that suggested, "Can you believe it?". He added, "Would you arrange for the funds to be settled and forwarded to us?"

It was John's turn to nod in the affirmative. He quickly added, "You know it's a significant amount, we're told the preliminary estimate from his attorney in Valencia...several million dollars!"

This got both of their attention. Les squeezed his arm involuntarily that seemed to be saying, I loved you as a poor retired federal/military employee, but I love you even more now. It may have been a broader interpretation than intended, but it clearly got their attention.

Jake regained his composure and responded cool and calm, "nevertheless, we'd appreciate it being the same way." Les loved how he used their names in a collective and cohesive manner, using the terms we and us, it made her feel even more secure in what could easily be described as a turbulent world for the two of them. Jake looked over at Les and commented, "That rascal."

Jake could not have dreamed what was about to happen next, and the impact it would have in his world beginning at this moment.

Chapter 28
A Life Changer

As Lieutenant Carter led them back to the main lobby Jake tried to make conversation with him. He asked, "Do you mind telling me what the K.D. stands for Lieutenant?"

He said, "No sir! I love telling this story. My father was a pilot in the war. He was shot down by a surface-to-air missile." Jake's radar began to ping. "My given name is Kevin Donald." Jake and Les stood in stark disbelief. Ironically, the bells from the cathedral they had just attended were beginning to ring in calling the faithful to 12 PM mass. Les could not resist, "You know every time a bell rings an angel gets his wings," a beautiful reference to the classic film, IT's A Wonderful Life...the sentiment was not lost on Jake.

Les gushed, "You're going to tell him, aren't you?"

A now solemn Jake, transitioning to Kevin mode stated, "My name is Kevin Flaherty."

K.D. stood in shocked disbelief looking back a Kevin and then Les. His expression almost read as if he were saying he could not believe it. He finally gathered himself and with a joy that came from deep from within his soul he exclaimed, "You saved my father's life, and in a way, you saved my life too." A small crowd looked on, K.D. pointed excitedly at Kevin and screamed again, "This man saved my father!"

Jake was becoming a memory now, still he did not appreciate the attention. He motioned K.D and Les to a semi-private alcove adjacent to the lobby. K.D. had a chance to gather himself and asked, "Do you remember my dad?"

Kevin smiled and responded somewhat sheepishly, "Sure, you never forget people you helped rescue. I recall your father being Thomas, is that right? And he was from Kansas?"

K.D. now grinning ear to ear and beginning to process the wonder of it all shook his head yes, "Yep, it's Tom Carter, and he still lives in Kansas."

"I was born almost nine months to the day he returned. He loved telling the story of his recovery, and gave you and Mr. Drake all the credit, said you were the bravest men he'd ever met."

Kevin was looking at his shoes and almost blushed in saying, "Well, I don't know about that..."

This was an opportunity for Les to join the conversation with, "Well I do, and yes he is!"

Kevin gained his composure and asked, "How's your Dad doing?"

K.D. enthusiastically, "Great and even better when he hears who I've met. Do you stay in touch with Mr. Drake?"

This last question turned the moment into a much more solemn discussion, Kevin managed to respond with, "Well no... not anymore. He recently passed away, but in the process may have helped to save our lives," gesturing at Les.

K.D. clearly saddened in a softer, more somber tone responded, "I am so sorry, and my father will be to, it sounds like he was a hero to the bitter end, just like all Marine's. Semper fi."

Kevin quietly rubbed his face and put his hand out Les, "Indeed, Semper, fi.

* Semper Fidelis, true meaning in Latin is 'Always Faithful, and is an oath taken by every Marine. It is a collective commitment to each Marine who fights alongside one another in battle, and in securing the success of those battles.

Intuitively, K.D knew he should not probe further, and ask, "I get off duty at 500 hours (shifting to military speak). would it be OK if I came over and bought you a drink?"

Collectively Kevin and Les nodded yes. It would be nice to have a little company. Little did they know that another old wound was about to be reopened.

Chapter 29
Confirmation

A moment before leaving the embassy a Marine orderly rushed to them shouting, "Sir, you forgot your newspaper." Jake, er Kevin now, reached out and took the paper thanking the young Marine.

Once inside the hotel they for two chairs in the far end of the lobby. Kevin opened the English version of the Valencia Olive Press, dubbed the best English newspaper in Spain. He was hoping to read the confirmation of Miles death. The article reads as follows:

The AP has reported that local authorities confirmed a shootout at a private residence in Valencia, involving Mexican nationals, believed to be a cartel member, and at least one American national occurred yesterday morning. The names of the Mexican nationals are not yet named due to delayed confirmation from the local consulate. The American national was identified as Miles Fender, a retired American entrepreneur who was living in Barcelona. It is unclear what his dealings with the Mexican nationals involved at this time, but the local American consulate has offered to assist in all matters involving the case.

Anyone attempting to find the former Miles Fender would believe he was deceased. Hopefully, the living members of the wounded cartel would see this as vengeance served. Both Sam and Miles had been eliminated, and hopefully this would discourage future efforts by authorities to disrupt their operations.

Kevin could not allow this attitude to persist and would make a point of demonstrating this on his terms. It was his priority, there were other fences to mend and recognition to current heroes to resolve, but he swore to himself there would be a reckoning.

Chapter 30
Any Cover is Good Cover

After confirming that the coverage of Miles demise was complete in the press, Kevin wanted to make sure additional steps were in place to assure the ruse was thoroughly established. His dealings with the embassy were all done under the guise of Jake and now Kevin.

He was also confident that the use of Leslie as a means of finding Miles was done. She had delivered Miles to them, Hector was no longer in play, and Sam's elimination was well documented. Kevin saw her as having no value to them unless they were even more vindictive than even, he could imagine.

He needed to close one more loop before he could truly take a deep breath and exhale. He called his trusted source within the "agency" and inquired how the investigation of Roosevelt Lincoln had come along. As suspected, he was found to be "dirty," and providing information to the cartel for large sums on cash considerations. It turned out Rosie had several vices that had led to his becoming vulnerable in this regard. Kevin's contact assured him Rosie had acted alone, was now in custody where he could no longer aid the cartel and would be tried for treason.

Kevin wondered aloud if there could be more value to a compromised Rosie. Could his connection to the cartel be used against them in a strategic and dramatic fashion? After conferring this idea with his contact, he left it in their capable hands. After all, he was retired, in Madrid with a beautiful woman and in love. They had a few hours before meeting Lieutenant Carter and plenty of clever ideas on how to spend them... "Just in case."

Chapter 31
Twisting the Knife

Almost 4500 miles away from Madrid, Special Agent Walker walked into a conference room in the Federal Correctional Institute in Seagoville, Texas. Rosie was in the room when he entered the room in shackles and flanked by two Federal Marshals. He looked about as low as a man could be, a high ranking and trusted member of a brotherhood of upper-level law enforcement officials who had gone bad and been caught. It was about to get worse, much worse.

Walker began with the unwelcome news, "Well, I thought you'd want to know your work with the bad guys is now complete...Miles and Leslie, along with another American national were killed by members of the cartel yesterday." He paused long enough for the words to fully sink in, and then followed through with, "So now we can connect your act of treason to four Americans, including Sam Grant."

Rosie was not sure if he should cry or vomit. He knew his actions could have consequences like this but had always somehow hoped that Miles would be clever enough to avoid this outcome after Sam was killed and Leslie sent to find Miles. As immortalized in the Eagles classic song, Tequila Sunrise... "When it comes down to dealing friends, it never ends." As with Eric Gibson before, when good people do bad things there is an attempt to rationalize their actions, but in this scenario, the death of multiple people he knew and cared about, it could never be rationalized, he had become the worst evil...a traitor.

Words began to sputter out of Rosie's mouth and bowed head, "I'm so sorry...I had no idea this would happen."

Walker erupted, "Don't give me that bullshit! You knew exactly what you were doing...exactly." Walker paced back and forth a couple of times before sitting back in his chair, he placed his elbows on the table separating them and leaned in, he had to admit he was now enjoying this role increasingly. In a much more even tone and looking directly into Rosie's eyes he nearly whispered, "If I had my firearm and these two Marshals weren't here, I'd shoot you myself." Again, Walker paused and then leaned back and added, "But I think that would be the straightforward way out for you. I will let you ponder the misery you've created. "Walker turned to the Marshals, "Take him back to his cell." Rosie walked out an utterly defeated man.

Walker was joined by Special Agent Withers, "Do you think he bought it? I know I did." Both agents were told this is what truly happened in Valencia. There could be no more leaks. Too much was at stake.

Chapter 32
Where Nightmares Come From

After an afternoon and early evening that could only be described as magical, including a siesta, Les and Kevin now headed toward the restaurant K.D. had suggested, Ten con Ten. When they arrived, they were surprised to find another young man with him. They were both in street clothes, but it was easy for anyone to recognize them as Marines in this case.

K.D. ushered them to the table and apologized for bringing his friend, Cpl. Mitch Travis, "I'm sorry, but when I shared our story with Mitch, he thought it sounded familiar, and you may have known his uncle."

Les and Kevin acknowledged the apology and agreed it would be fine. Kevin quickly added, "What is your uncle's name?" Assuming it was someone he had served with in the Corps.

When Mitch offered, "Pete Davidson." Kevin straightened up in his seat and squeezed Les' hand to a point that caused pain. This name hit a nerve for Kevin.

Mitch continued, "Uncle Pete said there was a man named Kevin who saved him when he was a POW in Laos." Kevin almost stood up to leave but couldn't react quickly enough.

The story went on, "You had just gotten released from solitary confinement and the prisoners were lined up for inspection by the commander. My Uncle was being hit for being 'insubordinate' or something," Mitch turned to Les and said, "My Uncle is only 5'7" tall." He turned back to Kevin and said, "You spoke up to the commander of the POW camp and shouted, "Why don't you pick on someone your own size. Needless to say, his full attention was drawn towards you and spared my uncle. It was not long after that the Camp was liberated. He said you were airlifted out first due to the injuries you received in protecting him. He never got to thank you."

All eyes now turned to Kevin and in an effort to lighten the mood he offered, "What can I say, I don't like bullies."

After a moment Kevin stood up and said, "Can you men escort Les back to the hotel? I need to take a walk."

Les jumped up, "I'm going with you." Kevin said in the most serious tone, "No, I need some time to myself. I will meet you back in the room. I'm sorry gentlemen."

K.D. and Mitch just stared at one another. They had been in such a rush to celebrate the heroism of a fellow Marine; they had conjured up memories that had been suppressed for years. They should have known better. Post-traumatic stress disorder (PTSD) was not as well defined or as easily diagnosed then as it was now, but they should have recognized how much Kevin had been through. They should have known better.

Les made it back to the hotel and their room and waited for what seemed an eternity.

Chapter 33
The Past Will Always Find You

Les had gotten back to the hotel with a sense of dread... "What if he needs my help? What if he's hurt? What if someone sees him in this emotional state and is unkind to him? What if he decides he can live without me and doesn't come back at all...just disappears?" Perhaps this was her greatest fear. Kevin had demonstrated the unique ability to just disappear in the past. In many ways he was part chameleon and part ghost. Who, if anyone would reappear tonight?

Her dread manifested itself in many ways. She paced around the suite so many times she thought the carpeting would be worn out. She tried to lay down, but felt she was hovering over the sheets. In the end, she poured herself a whiskey from the room bar, not because she liked or needed it, but because it made her feel closer to wherever Kevin was tonight.

In the end, she changed into one of his t-shirts and found a perch on the balcony, with her butt in the chair and feet on the railing she surveyed a large part of Madrid, its motto being, "*On water I was built, my walls are made of fire.*" He was out there, but where and most importantly, "Did he feel loved?"

Just then she heard the door opening. She desperately wanted to run to him but thought maybe it would be better if he found her, to leave the process in his hands. She felt his presence. She wished he'd say something or better yet throw his arms around her...what was taking him so long to find her? Oh, screw it, she jumped up and turned to see him.

What she saw shocked her. It was not the handsome man, the one with the kind eyes and the attitude he could do anything. It was a slightly hollowed up version of that same man who looked as though he'd gone 15 rounds with his own "ghosts."

He started with a soft, and more than heart felt apology, "I'm sorry. I'd hoped you'd never have to witness that, er this..."

gesturing to himself. "It's not something I usually want anyone to see, especially you..."

She couldn't stand it, she rushed into his arms and planted one of her famous soft and firm kisses on his lips and held it there for a much-extended time. She didn't want to give any indication off letting go. His lips tasted of whisky, tobacco and salt from the tears he had surely cried. She finally loosened her lips and the rest of her embrace slightly and held his face between her hands. He started to say something, and she quickly pressed the index finger of her left hand against his mouth, "You need to shut up and listen to something very carefully." She paused and nodded her head in the affirmative manner and Kevin instinctively nodded back. He'd seen glimpses of this woman before, and knew what she was about to say was really important, it was and she delivered her ultimatum in a near whisper, "OK? When I fell in love with you, I fell in love with the whole man, not just the man with happy memories. I fell in love with a man who made me feel safe, not just physically, but emotionally as well." While still holding his face she moved her hand to his chest and patted it while saying, "This man."

Kevin pulled back ever so slightly and began to say something, but once again her index finger found his lips, "Shhh, there's one more thing. I have this vision of intimacy in which I can tell you anything, my secrets and dreams, my hopes and fears...anything. The only catch is the shared intimacy needs to be a two-way street."

The two shared another nod that signaled agreement or buy-in. Kevin while still shaking his head in a positive fashion, "Can I say something?"

Les in a somewhat stern tone spoke directly while letting her hand fall from his face to around his wait, "Did you hear what I said?"

Kevin having waited his turn and with a half-smile said, "Yes, and they were the kindest words I've ever heard. If you really mean it, it could be a long night and a bumpy ride."

Les moved her hands from his waist to her hips, "Try me, I think you'll see I'm in it for the duration."

As Kevin removed his jacket and looked admiringly at Les, he never would grow tired of seeing her and the t-shirt was always a good start, he then spoke in a halting tone, "Well let's get started, but before we do... 'Just in case'."

As Les returned their now motto, "just in case." She pulled his t-shirt over her head. The lovemaking was intense and cathartic. It was full of joy, with just a touch of sadness. There were times when Kevin was the most grateful man in the world for all the gifts Les brought to him today, but still struggled with all the time he had missed.

As cathartic as the act had been, the conversation that followed would be even more so. Even though it was well past midnight, they moved out to their balcony, she back in his t-shirt and he in his boxers, and began the conversation he needed to say, and she needed to hear. They ultimately moved back into the bed, they left the balcony doors open there was a slight breeze that ruffled their curtains. Kevin propped himself against several pillows and he lay on her his chest, it was the most intimate moment either of them had ever experienced.

Chapter 34
Remorse Comes Hard

Meanwhile, back in Dallas a utterly remorseful Roosevelt Lincoln reflected just what his actions had caused...the death of two friends. Two people who had complete trust in him. As an "accomplice" to these phony murders, Rosie for some reason had never presumed the impact of his underhandedness, but it now was hitting him hard.

The death of his friends was bad enough. As with most villains, at least those with a conscience, the selfish thoughts came second. He began to wonder what the rest of his life would look like...a life in prison, viewed by family and friends/peers as a traitor or worse. His thoughts turned back to Eric Gibson, was his path the best way out of the misery that awaited him.

His thoughts were interrupted by another summons from Special Agent Walker. The man sitting across from Walker was clearly broken. As suspected, he had some conscience and they could use that, and he would also demonstrate the selfish trait to complete the task at hand.

Special Agent Walker began with a simple dagger to begin the proceedings, "Well, you must be proud of the results you've created here?"

Rosie lashed back with a bitter response, "You know how I must feel!"

Walker in a tone that was both judgmental and intentional in piling on the guilt replied, "Nope I have no idea." he paused for affect, "The idea of being a traitor to my country and responsible for the murder of two friends, two good people, one of which received the Medal of Honor from his country, it is really beyond my comprehension. It must feel pretty lousy."

Rosie slumped even further in his chair. He truly was a despicable person.

Walker sat back and watched a broken man dissolve further into an unknown depth of despair. He cautioned himself...you really shouldn't enjoy his work so much, but then was reminded of the man and his intentions. While Jake and Leslie had not been murdered, it could have been much worse had Jake not picked up on his unusual behavior during their phone conversation, as well as the heroic actions of Jake, Daf and Leslie in Valencia.

The torment in a situation that was confronting Rosie was useful to a trained agent. They could be as varied as the individuals being confronted. In this case Walker knew he had a good one. He spoke in measured tones, "We're sending for your mother, we thought you'd want to explain to her what you've done?" A sheer look of panic appeared on Rosie's face. Walker continued, "And just in case you try to sell her on the idea you did nothing wrong, we'll share with her the evidence we have on you. As you know, it's indisputable."

Rosie on the verge of a near and total breakdown sputtered, "You can't, it would kill her." and then in a whispered tone that was nearly unrecognizable, "It would break her heart."

Walker mustered up the cruelest version of himself responded, "A little late to think about that isn't it? He let the hit to the gut sit for a bit and then followed with, "Guess who gets to tell Jake and Leslie's parents. I do, and along with it I need to tell Jake's parents how a man he had considered a trusted friend had betrayed him for a few lousy bucks. Maybe your mother would like to apologize to them for her son's actions?"

Rosie bleated, "You wouldn't, you couldn't."

Walker now had him squared up this was going to be fun in a twisted, yet effective way, "Wouldn't I? Listen you son of a bitch. I have no use for you to begin with due to your actions, but Jake was a friend of mine, even more importantly I knew his record on behalf of being a true and selfless patriotic hero, there's nothing I wouldn't do to hurt you in any way I could, and I warn you, it's just beginning."

Rosie now sobbed, "Please...please, is there anything I can do, anything."

These were the words Walker wanted to hear. With the initial dagger inserted, Walker prepared to twist it hard. Every man or woman has their breaking point.

Chapter 35
Valley of the Fallen

S till in a somber mood Jake took Leslie on a scenic one-hour drive to a place he had visited before, the Valley of the Fallen. It is a monumental memorial to those who had perished during the Spanish Civil War and the combination basilica, monastery, cemetery and 500-foot Cross (the tallest in the world) is situated on 3600 acres (about half the area of Chicago O'Hare airport) of Mediterranean woodlands and granite boulders was intended was intended as atonement for those from both sides that were lost in the war.

Unfortunately, due to the fact the monument was constructed during the time was being ruled by the fascist dictator Franco it was not universally well received. There were serious claims made by the losing loyalists, including many Americans and popularized by Hemingway, that included those from the Catalan region, including Barcelona. Some of the most significant charges were the use of "slave labor" to build the memorial, in essence Loyalist prisoners were used in exchange for the time they were required to serve. Instead of the original intent it had become a lightning rod for both sides of the war.

Nevertheless, Kevin had always found it to be a fitting tribute for all casualties of war, and this was his third visit and something he wanted or needed to share with Leslie. In all wars there were what we considered "winners and losers," at least that is how the history books will read. In civil wars there were only losers and bigger losers. The "winners" in the Spanish Civil War ushered in a fascist regime in Spain, and permitted Germany, the emerging fascist regime and Hitler to supply weaponry to its and in many ways, field test them in this pre-WWII engagement. His personal war experience reinforced this notion of what war really meant.

Conversely, in all wars there those who acted nobly in horrendous conditions and others who prosecuted it differently. Unfortunately, this could occur on both sides, as demonstrated as far back as the Benedict Arnold story and now being revisited by Roosevelt Lincoln in a different scenario. Kevin was here with Leslie to honor people like Daf and others he had met personally in his journey, including Sam Grant. Those who had not been as fortunate as he was, especially now.

Taking the 'politics' out of the Valley of the Fallen development and which regime was responsible for the building process, it still did a nice job memorializing those who had made the ultimate sacrifice. While saying his prayer for the 'fallen' in his life, he promised Daf and others they would never be forgotten, and he would dedicate a large portion of his life making it so.

The memorial had an impact on Les as well. She had known several boys from high school who would never have the chance to complete their lives, and Sam was still foremost on her mind, even as her feelings for Kevin grew more intense. It was odd to think how rapidly she had been able to convert her feelings towards Kevin, and she wondered if her husband may have somehow intentionally placed the two of them within reach of one another. If so, it was truly one of the more selfless acts ever conceived.

Her brief affair with Hector still carried a blemish from her past life with Sam. As noted previously, it was a purely physical outlet during a difficult time in she and Sam's time together. She certainly was not proud of it, but the fact she had never uttered the words "I love you" at any point to him was a slight saving grace. The sex had been just OK, nothing like the feeling of being with someone you truly loved and cared about, nothing like what she had with Kevin.

Hector had paid the ultimate sacrifice for his dealings. The fact he had been killed by the very man she now loved seemed fitting in some way. Kevin, then Jake had warned her the shootout would "change her life" or at least part of it, and she grieved for Daf, but Hector had it coming, and she was happy to 'close the book' on any memories she had of him. She was confident they would stay in obscurity where they belonged. As far as the other men killed that day, they struck her as accomplices or 'bit players' in the saga for Kevin to escape being Jake and hopefully a return to a more normal, yet wonderful life together. Mission accomplished, she hoped.

On the ride back to Madrid in the Audi, Kevin shared not only his short-term plans, but how he was feeling towards her. Once again, he offered her an escape hatch, with the ability to step away from him for a brief period or longer, if needed. Les responded with a curt, "No thank you, you're stuck with me and please do not ever ask me that question again.

Kevin with a sense of relief added, "I was just saying..."

Again, a curt Les interrupted with, "And so am I, now knock it off! We need each other now." And she thought to herself 'forever', she hoped.

The visit to the Valley of the Fallen, the sharing of plans and his open description of his feelings towards her, fulfilled the sense of intimacy she craved. Could this euphoric feeling last? She certainly thought so, especially if they could keep each other alive. She knew that danger might show its ugly demeanor at almost any time.

As she felt the warm sun on her face and win in her hair she asked, "When do we leave for Florida?"

Kevin responded, "Tomorrow."

Her face changed into a sad pout, "Too bad, I liked it here. I'll never forget our time here."

Kevin concluded with, "So did I. I promise we will be back. Let's make tonight count."

Her pout changed into a devilish smile, and she added, "Oh, we will."

And they did.

Chapter 36
Can Bad People Do Good Things?

An ongoing debate continued in Dallas a thoroughly defeated man was now at his wits end and knew he was out of options. His former colleagues had caught him betraying his country and good friends. They were now threatening to expose his sins to his mother, who Rosie respected and loved more than anything in life. In fact, it was her encouragement that had led him to seek this role of service to the country and its citizenry, and now his evil behavior would be exposed.

A side of him wanted to say just shoot me. The outcome of the various charges could lead to an execution anyway...why not get it over with now and avoid further humiliation. His survival instincts were too strong, and he could not bring himself to requesting some form of an expedited end to what had become a tragic life.

He muttered a muted plea in the direction of Walker while not able to actually look him in the eye, "What can I do to keep my mother out of this mess?"

Walker absorbed the plea and almost seemed to chew on it for a while before responding with, "Well, I would describe it as a little more than a mess." He surveyed the scene in front of him before continuing with, "It's an absolute tragedy on so many fronts. Not only did you betray the people you had sworn to protect and did it with relish and thoroughness we rarely see from our enemies. It's like you took all the skills we had helped you develop and used them against us. I have never seen anything quite like it. It makes me wonder what would have happened if Jake hadn't alerted us to your behavior."

Rosie startled by the last sentence sat straight up in his chair and blurted out, What "unusual behavior?"

Walker responded in almost surgical precision and admiration for an operative who had been a real pro in this deadly game, "Jake said you were asking questions you already knew the answer to" pausing again to let the words settle in and continued with, "Almost like you were confirming a strike, and the saddest part of his observation was you were. He could have avoided it quite easily, but his loyalty to his friend and duty to his country forced him to stay targeted to help protect his friend's wife and his own death."

The last sentence was of course fiction. Rosie though had to now accept his own lack of judgement had led to his undoing, along with the intuition of a veteran operative. His defeat was now complete. He had nothing left but to beg for mercy or offer something more valuable than himself. In the end he would need to do both, and Walker knew it, even more than Lincoln.

Walker slyly added, "Well there might be something you could do for us. It would not reduce your sentence, but we would keep your mother out of this...as you call it mess and might ease your conscience a bit."

Rosie's only answer was, "I'll do anything!"

Chapter 37
Mas vale mana que fuerza/Better skill than strength

Their final night in Madrid was exactly what they both needed, and Jake thought to himself "I wish I could do that a million more times." They feasted on gazpacho, paella and of course sangria. They danced, Les was far better, but Jake made up for his shortcomings with enthusiasm. They walked back to the hotel arm in arm with an occasional pause to steal a kiss or two and enjoy the scenery of this beautiful city. While he had promised to bring Leslie back it was hard to predict when that would happen.

Jake kept figuratively pinching himself. Was this the way love was supposed to be? It was, but in this case, it was much better than most could hope for.

They made love in their suite. Again, with the balcony doors open wide and the curtains gently swaying with the breeze. This time it was less physical and cathartic and more soft, almost gentle. They were still getting to know each other's preferences and desires. Jake found kissing and caressing her shoulders and arms exquisite. Les had a very athletic body that was still 100% feminine. He thought she was the most striking woman he had ever met when everything was taken into consideration.

The next morning a thoroughly rested and content couple boarded the Air France Airbus 380 for the first leg of their trip... there were no direct flights from Madrid to Gainesville. The Airbus 380 is a magnificent ride once airborne, it appeared ungainly on the tarmac, and his new friends in the diplomatic corp under instruction from the highest sources within the intelligence and justice communities, had authorized first class accommodations. Neither of them had ever traveled first class and they felt almost like two kids on their honeymoon.

As they approached the US coast, and their connection at JFK, they began to think about what lay ahead. The next phase of their journey was intended to repair some damage from what had seemed a lifetime ago. As referenced previously, there were some ghosts in Jake, now Kevin's past that needed exorcising, and he was committed to making it happen.

The plane arrived @ 2 PM and they decided to check in at the Double Tree first.

By the time they were ready to make their first stop it was nearly 4 PM. Kevin had rented a car and knew the address by heart. The city had not changed much since he last saw it. Although he was certain it had in many ways, especially from his perspective. He was a more worldly citizen of the world today, but there is always a longing for 'home' in each of us

Kevin had left Gainesville and idealistic young man, who had enlisted in the Marines as a sense of fairness towards other young men who had not been provided his options. His life experiences, first as a Marine, and then the role he had been asked to play as an operative for the agency. Both experiences had 'hardened' him, but had also created a vulnerability that he was now beginning to understand thanks to his relationship with Leslie

As he pulled up to the modest ranch style home Les squeezed his hand, "Shall I accompany you?"

A nervous and focused Kevin responded with, "I don't think so, you better let me handle the first step by myself. I'll call you in shortly for reinforcements."

He took a deep breath and held it before stepping out of the car. She smiled and nodded and could barely release his hand. These next moments were his first real look into his past and what could have been Kevin walked to the front door and rang the bell. After a few moments, the door opened and a man in his early sixties opened it. The man standing before him looked familiar in a mysterious, almost magical way. Jim Flaherty caught himself staring and shook his head, trying to shake loose the cobwebs of the late afternoon nap he had just awoken from, "I'm sorry, can I help you?"

He was still struggling with the recognition of who was standing before him when Kevin commented, "I hope so, Dad."

Chapter 38
Setting the Trap

Rosie was now prepared to act on their behalf in crippling the cartel once again, and Walker knew it. Above being one of the FBI's best interrogators, Walker had advanced degrees in Criminal Psychology at UC, Irvine and an advanced degree in Forensic Psychology from John Jay University (SUNY), and more importantly "the school of hard knocks" over the last 20 years in the field. He was certainly one of the best and brightest in the Bureau. However, the stakes in this case were particularly high, not only was the potential prize significant, but it would also be putting other agents and local law enforcement in harm's way...never to be taken lightly.

Rosie, the linchpin for the entire operation, had been taken into custody under the tightest of security measures. There had been a sense of his becoming an asset for the Bureau. His direct involvement in the killings of Sam Grant, a revered member of the FBI and former Texas Ranger, and Miles Fender, a less widely known undercover operative, but key in the damage done to the cartel, had placed Rosie in good stead with his new bosses, as well and swelled his overseas bank accounts with seven figures in "bonuses."

These accounts were now in Federal custody, the residual effect was the "good guys" would be receiving additional payments for setting a trap against the cartel itself. Rosie himself was now learning in the hardest way possible that money would not buy happiness, and a guilty conscience...at least he had one for the killing of Sam and feigned killing of Miles, would haunt him for the rest of his life His final act on behalf of the "good guys" would help to assuage these horrible feelings to some degree or maybe not.

They had rehearsed the call dozens of times, and Walker along with a team of FBI communication experts would monitor the call to ensure its completeness and accuracy, as well as voice recognition or any clues to where the recipient was located. These efforts were certainly linked to the primary operation but were not expected to produce much in the way of results. Rosie had only known his contact as Patron, his code name was Longhorn, in reference to his college football team.

The line went live...

Patron began with, "Hola Longhorn."

Longhorn countered with, "Hello Patron. Were you happy with the outcome of our latest transaction?"

Patron in a positive manner, "Si, Bueno. Muy bien. We lost some valuable assets, but the elimination of Señor Fender was worth it. Did you receive your payment?"

Longhorn was now more business like, "Yes, but I may have a bigger opportunity for us."

A curious Patron, "Bueno, tell me more."

Longhorn planting the seed, "The FBI is planning a memorial for Sam Grant. The event will draw a large contingency of FBI, DEA and some VIP's. It could be a perfect target for you to deliver a final knockout. You'll never see this many high level law enforcement in a specific location. I'm going to want to double my normal payment."

A now anxious Patron responded, "OK, no problem. What type of VIP's?

In his most sincere voice Longhorn announced, "The Vice President of the United States!"

Patron gushed, "Muy bien, Donde esta?"

Longhorn replied sternly, "The Alamo!"

As they wrapped up the call the communication expert motioned Walker over.

Walker anxiously, "What is it?"

The expert excitedly, "Patron."

Walker hurriedly, "What about him?"

The expert, "We know who he is, and..."

Walker, "And?"

The expert, "He's in country."

Walker allowed his thoughts to wander a bit...this could be an even bigger opportunity than he imagined.

Chapter 39
The First Homecoming

After greeting a visitor at his front door in a casual manner, he had suddenly realized who was standing in front of him...

You could have knocked Jim Flaherty over with a feather. His startled mind automatically flashed back to the last time he had seen Kevin, a much younger man in his prime, and compared it to the man standing before him. It didn't take too much imagination to recognize them as the same person. All he could muster as he reached out to embrace his son was, "Kevin?"

Now in a firm embrace and clapping each other on the back as men do when hugging one another, Kevin uttered, "I'm sorry. I am so sorry."

His father in a mixture of sobbing and laughing held him out so he could have a more thorough look at him replied, "Nonsense! You're here and alive that's all that matters." He shook his head in almost disbelief and continued, "I'll be darned, I can't believe it. Please come in."

Kevin asked, "Is it OK if I bring someone else in?" After his father nodded yes, he motioned for Les to join them. He introduced her with, "Dad you might remember Leslie Richardson from high school?"

To which his father replied, "Well yes, maybe. Regardless, it's wonderful to meet you on this special day."

Les responded with, "It's an honor, sir."

Jim waved her off with, "It's Jim, nobody has called me sir since I quit teaching at the University." He followed with, "Are you two...?"

Les blushed and Kevin responded, "No, not yet we've only recently reconnected...it's a bit of a long story, and we've got a lot to catch up on." Jim shook his head and smiled, "We sure do."

It warmed Les to hear the words 'not yet'. While things were happening at a rapid pace, she had quietly thought to herself that this would be the eventual outcome for the two of them. She was still grieving over the loss of Sam, and it was almost impossible to believe she had fallen for Jake, now Kevin this quickly. The events surrounding their "courtship" had a lot to do with her falling so hard for Kevin and she hoped with all her heart Sam would understand.

As they moved to sit around a table that seemed to double as both a kitchen and dining area, Kevin continued to eye the home's interior suspiciously, he remembered the house as being "neat as a pin" when he was growing up. As they settled in and before Kevin began with the details behind his "reincarnation" he asked hesitantly, "Where's Mom?"

Jim immediately shook his head, looked downward, and said simply, "I don't know." Kevin listened and waited. The response could be construed as either she was running an errand or had passed away. Reluctantly his father continued, "After we received notice of your death things got really hard. We held a memorial. It was well attended, with lots of fellow Marines, pilots who said you had rescued them and all. We were immensely proud, but incredibly sad. You were our pride and joy." He paused and looked at Kevin and Les, she had begun to tear up thinking how sad it must have been losing a child.

Kevin took it all in more stoically but shook his head and repeated, "I'm sorry, I am so sorry."

His father dismissed his apology with, "Nonsense, I'm sure it wasn't your fault." He paused again before continuing with, "Your Mom could not accept you were gone...and" motioning to Kevin "turns out she was right. She tried to find you or proof you were really gone. Eventually, after a few years, she gave up hope and decided to dedicate her life to what you would have wanted her to do."

Kevin sat in silence and tried to absorb everything that was being said. He was beginning to understand how much of a void his loss had created much like the other scenes from It's a Wonderful Life. The removal of a single person can change lives, alter history and the re-entry has no guarantee of setting things right for all participants like in the dramatic and romantic films of his youth. He preferred the reference of the bell ringing in Madrid. This re-entry was going to be much harder than he thought.

Chapter 40
The List

As Kevin helped to fill in the blanks of a life interrupted, he had to be careful not to say too much, and he purposely left his operational name, Miles Fender out of it. Anyone related to that name would immediately have enemies, and after everything else his family had endured, any additional harm was unthinkable.

His father explained that after her initial search for Kevin, she began volunteering at the VA hospital in Gainesville. She felt serving veterans is what Kevin would have wanted her to do. One thing had led to another, she obtained an advanced degree in Public Health at the University of Florida, and quickly moved from volunteer, to employee, to department head and was now running a region for them in Colorado. It would have been a "fairy tale" story of a successful career rise if not for what had initially driven her to the field. Nevertheless, Kevin could not help but feel a sense of pride in hearing of her accomplishments.

As the night wore on, Kevin asked if his boot locker had ever been returned to the family. He was thrilled to find it had. In opening it he began to shudder, it was as if he was opening a "Pandora's box" of memories, some good and a few bad. In it he found a uniform, some medals, and ribbons, they were not what he was looking for. In the very bottom of it was a worn and faded manila folder. As he pulled it out, he asked his father if he could have it, his father nodded and said, "The way I see it all belongs to you now."

After assuring his father they would return tomorrow for breakfast, his father initially offered them to stay, they returned to the Double Tree. He asked his father to keep this news to himself for the time being. Both he and Les' heads were spinning with what they had found and learned that evening. Kevin had begun his reintroduction to the real world. In the room now Kevin pulled the manila folder out and opened it slowly. In it was a collection of letters and a list. The list totaled 29 names, there were 25 on the first and four on the second. Les asked tentatively, "Who are these people?"

Kevin clearly moved stammered, "Well...well the first 25 are the ones we saved, and..." Kevin could not say the words.

Les let it settle in and then finished the sentence, "The ones you didn't?"

Kevin could only nod his head yes and had begun to cry. After comforting him with a long embrace Les asked if she could look at the letters. Again, Kevin nodded yes, and this time stood up and walked to the window. Les proceeded to read each letter to herself, each one impacting her harder than the last. The letters were an apology to the families of the men he couldn't save from the list. In it were lines such as "I tried my best," "I wished I could have done more" and in the last letter an unbelievable line that read, "I'll never forgive myself."

She carefully put everything in place and put the folder down. She walked over and put her arms around Kevin from behind and whispered, "Sweetie, you did everything you could."

As Kevin turned to face her in their embrace he gestured to the folder and muttered, "Clearly I didn't, or I had not needed to send those letters."

She wanted to say a lot of things, but chose to say nothing, the two of them holding each other at that moment said it all and more. She had learned what defined the man, she had a feeling that somehow this investigation of his past would determine what he, and hopefully they, would do together.

Chapter 41
The Cause

By the time Kevin and Les reconnected with his father for breakfast Kevin had sent "the List" to his contact within the Agency. He requested contact information, as well as much of a bio on each member as was available. Kevin knew these 25 names would play a key role in what his plans were.

After an enjoyable morning that included additional conversation on what had transpired in Kevin's original community in Florida during his absence, what some of his old friends were up to, who had thrived in their lives and a few who had not. It was beginning to get easier to talk with his dad about their current situation, but the updates on some of his "friends and family" served as a reminder to Kevin of what he had sacrificed for his country and others. He clearly had some catching up to do.

He also sensed his father had become rudderless in dealing with his life after Kevin was reported KIA. He and Kevin's mother did not have other children to focus on, and clearly, they had both reacted differently in how they chose to deal with it. His father's early "retirement" from a once rewarding career as a college professor had several years of uninspiring work demonstrated how lost he had become. His father before Kevin's departure had been a bright, inspiring and relatively young professor. He deserved more, and Kevin had just the right idea for it.

They paused for a moment in their reminiscing, Kevin looked over at Les and winked, she knew what he was about to say, and Kevin chose the words he was about to say carefully:

"Dad, we need your help. Les and I want to start a foundation on the part of a fallen friend and hero, and we'd like you to be the Executive Director. The name of the Foundation is the Donald ((Daffy) Drake Memorial Fund. It will be partially funded by assets from his estate ($2 million) and Les and I will sit on the Board you establish and be your chief fundraisers. The Fund will have a goal of contributing 20% of its assets annually to either the Wounded Warriors or POW/MIA associations. Both goals can be recalibrated based upon your input and recommendation to the Board for consideration. Your starting base salary will be $75,000 plus expenses. What do you think?"

Kevin had phrased these words so that his father would feel needed and to explicitly state that he and Les would-be part of it...his additional means of keeping her in his life.

Kevin's father was caught off-guard to say the least, his awkward response was "Gee, I don't know. I have never done anything like this before. What if it turns out I do not like doing it? I just do not know if I am ready for this yet."

Kevin let the words sink in and then added, "Well, first, Les and I spoke, and we cannot think of anyone better to do the job. Plus, we will stay connected through our Board presence and fundraising activity...in fact we're kicking off our first campaign later in the week, so you are going to get started with licensing, bank accounts and whatever else you need to run things. We expect to make our first donations within the year." He sensed some continued reluctance with, "Dad, I will never ask you to do anything you are not capable of and this project is extremely important to both Les and me. Here is the deal, if you decide after the first six months you do not like what you are doing you can withdraw as soon as you hire your replacement. However, I think you are going to like it, and I know you're up to the task."

Kevin had instilled in his verbal offer to his father three critical components: 1) He (Kevin) needed help, 2) it was an important and worthy endeavor, and finally 3) he was "up to the task." Again, Kevin let his words hang there, and Les smiled at his father and nodded yes to encourage him to accept it.

Finally, his father blurted out, "OK, for the two of you and Donald the answer is yes!"

Kevin smiled and held out his hand to 'shake on it', the only words uttered were "We call him Daf." He turned to hug Les and whispered in her ear, "I'm so happy." All she could manage was, "I know, so am I."

They spent the remainder of the day planning and setting expectations for the short and long-term goals needed. for the DDMF, as it would now be referenced as, to 'hit the ground running.' They ordered pizza from the place Kevin remembered. He provided some background to his father on Daf, but excluded the specifics on his recent demise.

Finally, he and Les got up and said they had an early flight to catch but would be back in a few days and would check in by phone at least daily. Kevin also promised to have the initial fundraising campaign begun by week's end. There was no time to waste. He also asked if he could keep word on his return private for now. Kevin wanted to manage it and was afraid some media outlet might find out and run with it.

His father asked, "Where are you headed?"

Kevin answered, "Denver. I have someone I need to see."

Kevin's father managed a sly smile, and said simply, "Give her my best."

By the time Kevin and Les returned to the hotel there was a package waiting for him. It was the contact information and bios he had requested.

Les remarked, "That was fast."

Kevin responded with, "It's nice to have friends in high places."

As they entered the room and closed the door Les in an unconvincing tone suggested, "You must be tired?"

Kevin with his own sly grin answered, "Not that tired." It was not quite Spain with the curtains blowing from the warm breeze and the complete newness of the relationship, but Kevin was beginning to understand if she was there, he was as happy and content as he ever had been.

Plus, most of the nightmares were gone as well. On this night he would dream of his mother. The strong woman he had left behind. How would she respond to his sudden and inexplicable return? He would know soon enough.

Chapter 42
Ambush

There are several key elements that go into a successful ambush, including a complete surprise, overwhelming weapons superiority and an enemy that was over-confident. Walker felt he had all three, and was anxious to engage the enemy, but not too anxious.

Patron was swelled with confidence after several recent engagements had gone in their favor and had no reason to doubt his intelligence. He was imaging how another tremendous perceived victory would factor into his status within the cartel. He had gone one further in renting a helicopter to survey his handiwork following the decisive victory.

On the ground was Oscar Fuentes, driver of the first truck. He knew as a long time mercenary that things were never as easy or simple as they would appear. His premonition was about to come true.

Engaging foreign born national who are armed on US soil created the leeway necessary for this mission. The FBI's Mission Statement read simply, "To protect r\the American people and the US Constitution." This intentional ambiguity provided the guidelines necessary to complete this task. The FBI had their own SWAT teams in every office, and usually they were sufficient for any activity, but this action required support from the Texas National Guard. The Guard had their own Special Forces in the world of Green Berets to be deployed alongside the FBI, as well as the RPG's (rocket propelled grenades) that were necessary to disable the trucks being used by the attacking force.

Walker held his breath and whispered into the headset, "Engage!"

Oscar caught a glimpse of the RPG prior to its hitting the midsection of his truck. Half the occupants were killed instantly, and the other half were fully disoriented and could not return fire. Most of them were now being targeted by the FBI snipers.

The second and third trucks swerved to avoid the first truck. The occupants rushed to evacuate from their vehicles, sensing the same outcome that had befallen their stricken comrades. Nearly half were immediately taken down by snipers. The mercenaries knowing, they were in a real mess now, and that their only way out was to surrender.

The driver of the fourth truck made the mistake of trying to escape. No sooner had it made its attempted U-turn, as another RPG smashed into the real of the vehicle, killing a third of the occupants. The remainder exited with their arms rising in clear surrender.

Walker looked at his watch. the initial ambush took less than 3 minutes to conduct, and all that was left was clean-up. The helicopter pilot with Patron above the carnage that had been a group of expensive, highly trained mercenary force, now noticed an Apache alongside him. The Apache pilot was indicating the other needed to land. While his defeated occupant urged the pilot to take evasive maneuvers, the pilot knew there was no outrunning an Apache, it was over.

Chapter 43
"You Can Do Anything."

As they prepared to board the plane to Denver, they were no longer authorized to fly first class, like the flight from Madrid a few days earlier, but the Delta Airbus 321 was a comfortable plane in any seat assignment, and the conversation focused on his father's reaction to the "Kevin miracle" as Les like to refer to it as.

Les went first, "Well, I do not think it could have gone any better. Your dad is clearly excited about having you back in his life, and you also gave him a purpose."

Kevin interjected, "First of all I don't see any of this being me or you are doing something, it always needs to be 'our, we or us'. Does that make sense? I know right now I'm kind of hogging all the attention, but you're my partner...everything we accomplish moving forward is due to 'our' efforts."

Once again, Les had that warm feeling she received every time Kevin described a future with her in it. She didn't want to imagine a world without him in it. She sensed, with his continued emphasis on "us" that he must feel the same way. Les followed up with, "You think he's up to the task of being the Executive Director? It's a pretty big deal, especially with the start-up elements."

Kevin being serious, "I know so. The father I knew as a kid growing up could have done this job with one hand tied behind his back and while multi-tasking other independent issues. He just needed a nice kick in the butt to begin with...he'll do fine. Besides, I'm not sure you'd like who my second choice was."

A more interested Les responded, "Who?"

Kevin looking absently off in the distance, "You...he left the word hang by itself."

Les in her serious mode, "Me, I don't know anything about running a non-profit memorial fund. Plus, if I'm doing that, I may not be able to travel and be with you." Now in a coyer manner, "Wouldn't you miss me?"

Kevin nodding said, "Well of course I would, but we'd find a way, we always do. As far as the job goes you would be terrific. I'm beginning to think you can do anything." It was a nice sentiment. Kevin went on to say, "I was also concerned with the look of impropriety and/or conflict of interest. It's one thing to have your father involved, his reputation is beyond reproach, but to have the woman I'm sleeping with...well I don't know. It sounds a little fishy."

Les immediately slapped his arm/shoulder, "Kevin is that who I am, just a woman you're sleeping with?"

Kevin concluded, "Well, I'm not sure how much sleep we're getting." Les slapped the same spot, this time even harder. He grew serious once again, "Les, you're the love of my life. I cannot imagine not being with you, in the immortal words of Smokey Robinson, 'You really got a hold of me.'"

Les sat back and mused, "Just the way I like it."

Next, Kevin decided to approach his mother on a more direct basis. Of the two parents Kevin had, she was the stronger of the two. Let there be no question, Kevin loved his father, but his fondness and respect was more greatly piled on with her, and not him. He silently hoped that everything would go well.

Finally, he worked on a letter to be sent to the 25 men on the list, the other four would require a personal visit. The first draft read as:

Dear _____,

I hope this letter finds you well...if you're receiving it, we have something, we all knew, respected and in my case loved Donald (Daffy) Drake. As a helicopter pilot, we partnered in saving 25 men from imprisonment or worse. It was more recently, several weeks ago in which Daf performed another heroic act, this time I was the recipient of the sacrifice he made.

I think of each and every one of you often, it was always my dream, that not only would Daf and my actions return that person to his friends and family, but that each one of you would make a difference in the lives of others within your community. I know this will turn out to be accurate and will make a point of hearing your stories.

Leslie Richardson and I have taken steps to create the Donald (Daffy) Drake Memorial Fund. The Fund will provide the following organizations Wounded Warriors and POW/MIA with sustainable funds to rehabilitate, educate and celebrate their lives. We've seeded our Fund with monies received from Daf's estate. This $2 million gives us a running start, but we need more to meet our complete goals.

I am therefore asking you for two things, 1) Can you commit to an annual donation to keep Daf's memory and do good for those who may have fallen along the way, and 2) if you would offer to become a designated fundraising champion in your region and on our behalf.

In closing, I am a better man for knowing Daf, and the only way I can directly thank him comes from our ability to keep his memory alive in all of us. Please do whatever you can to support us.

Respectfully yours,
    Kevin Flaherty
    Lieutenant, US Marines (retired)
    SEMPER FI

Chapter 44
A Four Point Swing

A common phrase from his basketball playing days, when your adversary misses a seeming lay-up, and you immediately take advantage of it and score two points on your own. As Special Agent Walker surveyed the scene, he could not help but feel an enormous sense of relief and pride.

First, in executing the dramatic and risky action on American soil, it had worked as well if not better than hoped. They had drawn the cartel onto the battlefield, and in so doing crippled their ability to operate within their sphere of influence. This 'sphere' sent immense amounts of illicit drugs, human trafficking, money laundering and other nefarious activities against the US and its citizens. Unfortunately, this powerful cartel, as wounded as they were would ultimately 'reload' or be replace by another equally powerful entity. And most importantly, not a single loss of life.

Secondly, the memory of Sam and Miles, and the revenge for their heroic deaths had been exacted. Walker wished more could be shared on the heroic actions of these two brave American's. If he, had it his way there would be monuments for each of them to remind the rest of us of the sacrifices being made each day on our collective behalf.

He allowed himself one more thought, he smiled and said one last "thank you" to the two departed heroes. They both would have wanted it this way.

He had one last step to close, he had promised the head of the 'agency' a report after the outcome of the action. He began his report with...

Mission Accomplished Final Score: 16 bad guys KIA, injured or captured, four suburban trucks demolished, and one extremely high leader captured and showing signs of cooperating with authorities.

Chapter 45
Partial Closure

Immediately after landing in Denver Kevin's phone rang. There had been several missed calls, but there was no way this message could be left on voicemail. Kevin answered and was immediately briefed on the results of the action, including the capture of El Patron. This part of the entire action, if Patron could be turned, would become the most beneficial element of the entire victory moving forward.

Kevin hung up the phone, turned to Les, and smiled, "We got 'em!" Later, once they had left the airport and located their rental car Kevin explained all the details. The using of Rosie to set up the cartel, the Alamo as the site of the action, and the complete victory against the people who had been responsible for the killing of Sam and Daf.

The revenge factor was not lost on Les. She immediately thought of her gallant and wonderful husband, Sam, and their friend, Daf. As always, she felt a tinge of guilt for being a survivor of the entire saga and her relationship with Kevin. She still believed in her heart that it was meant to be, and somehow Sam had actually put it all in motion for the two of them.

After an extended period of silence in which she reached over and grabbed Kevin's hand and said, "Promise me."

Kevin, "What? Anything."

Les in a pleading manner, "That you'll stay retired."

Kevin hesitated and then followed with, "I'd like to, but..."

Les interrupted, "But what? You've done enough, and...and I couldn't bear to lose you."

Finally, Kevin responded with a gentle squeeze of her hand, "I know, and believe me, I have every intention of staying 'retired'. Just as I did in Barcelona, but then you came into my life."

Les smiled and said, "I bet you wished you hadn't taken that call. You'd still be back in that beautiful city beating off all those senoritas with a stick."

Kevin concluded, "I wouldn't change a thing, except for Daf. As far as I'm concerned, I won the biggest lottery of my life with you, and I intend to keep it that way."

Les blushed with that warm overall feeling that Kevin was so good at creating. She also knew that there had been no absolute promise made today. She decided to hold onto that for now and address it later when she had more leverage. She smiled thinking when that time might be.

Kevin cleared his head and began thinking of the task at hand. He needed to reintroduce himself to his mother.

Chapter 46
No Other Way

Kevin had decided to take the direct approach with his mother. He did not have a home address and could not even imagine doing something like this over the phone or via a letter. It had to be done face-to-face.

He asked Les for input and she concurred. Her feminine intuition also led her to recommending she not be in the room at the time...as much as she wanted to be, for fear that somehow his mother may conclude she had more to do with his absence from her life. It was agreed she'd wait in the lobby for as long as it took. She needed to be there, just not in the room.

Kevin approached the Receptionist, "I'm here to see Elizabeth Flaherty."

The Receptionist asked, "Do you have an appointment?" Knowing full well he didn't.

Kevin responded, "No, but I know she'd like to see me."

The intercom buzzed in her office, "There's a gentleman to see you..."

In hearing the name over the intercom her heart stopped. Over the year's whenever she heard the first name Kevin she'd immediately thought of her son and tried to imagine him. Unfortunately, or maybe fortunately, the dead never age, so she had always remained as she last knew him. Oh, she often wondered what he would have become, but then needed to flush these thoughts from her mind...it was just too painful. All of these thoughts were compressed into her mind when the Receptionist said the name. She had even met another Kevin Flaherty before and was sure this was just another coincidence... "Send him in."

She rose to greet her "visitor" and wondered if she should share the 'coincidence' with him. The door opened and she was stopped in her tracks. The appearance was startling, this could be an older version of the boy she'd loved as her only son, only child.

She momentarily reached over and grabbed the corner of her desk, and then realized if she had not her legs would not have allowed her to remain standing. In gathering herself and her composure she spoke in an apologetic tone, "I'm sorry Mr. Flaherty, but you have a strong resemblance to..."

Kevin could not stand back from the woman who had loved him first, the person who was most responsible for who he was, "Mom, it's me!"

A euphoric feeling overwhelmed her, and yet she couldn't erase all the sadness that had accompanied her these many years. In many ways it was the best/worst emotion you could imagine feeling. She straightened herself and said plainly, "And so it is."

The awkward moment passed, and they moved towards each other, her reticence of being sure it really was him, and his sensing how difficult this was for her. They finally came together, and Kevin said the same words he spoken two days earlier to his father, "I'm sorry."

As the tears began to flow his mother released him only to grab his face between her hands and say, "Is it really you?"

Kevin took a step back and nodded yes. He followed with another, "I am so sorry, you must have a thousand questions, and I'm sure I have 1001 answers. I just had to come see you."

In gathering herself a bit more she asked, "Does your father know?"

Kevin, "Yes, we saw him two days ago, and he told us where you were and what you were doing."

She quickly asked, "How is he doing?"

Kevin's response, "He's doing fine and filled me in on the two of you. Again, I am so sorry, I know my actions are directly responsible for this happening. And yes, someone came into my life recently that helped all of this to happen."

His mother now regaining her footing a bit more managed, "Well, whoever they are, I'm grateful to them for this." She went over to her intercom and spoke again to the Receptionist, "Please reschedule my meetings and hold all my calls for the rest of the day"

The Receptionist acknowledged, "Will do, even Secretary Gamble?"

Being reminded of her appointment for drinks with the Secretary of Health and Human Services she replied, "No, I'll call him myself." She grabbed her purse and motioned to the door, "We have some catching up to do."

They certainly did.

Chapter 47
She 'Saved' Me

After meeting Leslie in the Reception Area, they took the elevator down to the Valet in the garage. A bright shiny Audi A8 was brought up and Kevin and Les smiled at one another in seeing the coincidence in their taste in cars. Elizabeth drove towards her town home in town and along the way asked Les, "So how do you know my son?"

Liz paused, seeking approval in the form of a nod from Kevin, "Kevin was a friend of my deceased husband." She was not sure what else should say, but settled on, "He saved me."

Kevin immediately interrupted with, "In reality, she saved me."

Elizabeth mused, "It sounds interesting."

The rest of the afternoon was spent filling in the blanks of a life interrupted, while intentionally leaving out many of the details. The high points being his survival from being a POW and the cruel treatment he'd received. To his recruitment into clandestine operations and some of the recent steps that had led him into "retirement" and ultimately to her again.

He spent additional time describing the creation of the Foundation. His father's new position and the list. During this portion of the story his mother muttered, "Good old fashioned Irish Catholic guilt. It's a powerful motivator."

Towards the end of his story his mother said the obvious, "I understand and am prouder of you than ever, but still can't understand why you couldn't tell us you were alive?"

Kevin anticipated the question and responded, "I had already wrecked your lives once. The likelihood of me surviving in my recent role was 50/50 at best, more likely 25/75. The thought of doing it to you a second time was unacceptable. Additionally, the agents with families were more 'distracted' at times, and as evidenced by Les and her husband's story, loved ones can be used against us. Our enemies in the world I was living in our ruthless and would not stop at anything to gain an upper hand. My alias needed to die for me to be able to walk away."

His mother nodded, "It's flawed logic, but I guess we live in a deeply flawed world. The important thing is you're hear now and let's make the best of it."

The last phrase resonated with both Kevin and Les as they looked at one another Kevin responded, "Indeed, let's make the best of it."

Chapter 48
Anything

Elizabeth Flaherty began to process everything Kevin was telling her. It was a convoluted tale with a great many missing parts. She thought to herself, "My therapist will have a field day with all this information." Tucked into everything she had absorbed that day was the enormous joy that her son was still alive. He had served his country with valor and honor, as far as she knew, and it was now their collective turn to reap what had been owed them.

Near the end of Kevin's saga she asked, "How's your dad?"

Kevin took a breath, smiled and then said in a serious tone, "Well, I guess about the same. He had something taken from him that was now coming back. I suppose it is a mixture of happiness and additional sadness in knowing something was out there, yet untouchable, until now. Oh, and he likes his new job." Looking over at Les with the last comment.

Elizabeth smiled and said, "I need to call him. You know I never stopped loving him. We just could not be together anymore. We wanted different things in your closure."

Kevin apologizing once again, but with a little sense of hope for the future responded, "I am so sorry. He said pretty much the same thing."

Elizabeth's mood switched immediately, "Well, you must do me one favor!"

Kevin without thinking it through and in wanting to please his mom almost shouted, "Anything!"

In a delighted manner she added, "I'm meeting a friend tonight and want to introduce him to both of you. After all, this is the new happiest day of my life."

Kevin, not wanting to disappoint his mother in any way managed a less enthusiastic, "Ok."

Elizabeth gushed, "You'll love him! He's a former US Senator who is now the Secretary of Health and Human Services, Anson Gamble."

Kevin with clear trepidation in his voice gathered himself, "I am sure we will, but there need to be some ground rules...nothing about my past can be revealed. "Understood?"

His mother, now giddy responded with, "He's 100% trustworthy. After all, he's a former US Senator."

Kevin managed an "Of course." He thought to himself, never say 'anything' again, particularly in advance of a favor being asked.

Elizabeth finished with, "Meet us at the Oxford Hotel Bar at 7 PM tonight."

Chapter 49
"What is the Worst that Could Happen?"

Kevin left his mother's home with conflicted feeling on how the afternoon had gone. Clearly, the overall reintroduction of him into her life went as well as could have been expected, but the last piece of the conversation left him unsettled at best. He knew better than to put a "mission" at risk to make another party happy, but the circumstances here were unique to say the least.

Leslie had to chime in, "I wish you'd stop beating yourself over this situation. I'm sure it will be fine."

All Kevin could muster was, "What if it isn't?" The first rule of a field operative was to try and not take an unforeseen risk, especially if it involved another operative. He had violated both principles. In a non-operative world, he used to think in terms of, 'What is the worst that could happen' as a deciding factor in decision-making, but once those options became 'Someone could die', it was no longer used as a determinant.

Les continued, "For crying out loud, the man's a former US Senator and now holds a cabinet position that reports to the President."

Kevin decided to defer from further agitation with his partner, "Well, that's kinda what concerns me. They're known to have 'loose lips', especially if it's something that could help them look good, but what's done is done and I could never disappoint my mom now."

His phone buzzed and he noted it was his dad. Kevin thought...pretty good timing. He answered, "Hi Dad."

His father in a voice that held renewed vigor responded, "Kevin my boy, how are you and Les doing?"

Kevin responded, "Pretty good, we just left mom's place."

His father in a more measured tone asked, "How'd she take it? How's she doing?"

Kevin speculated a bit in saying, "I think as well as can be expected. She says she is going to call you. Just one hitch though..."

Suddenly his father blurted out, "I have to let you go, she's calling "Before Kevin could respond the line went dead.

His father answered the next call with a "Liz, can you believe it? Our prayers were finally answered."

Liz wanted to say, 'What did prayers have anything to with it'. She had long ago given up on religion to help her through her bitter adult life, but just maybe there was something to it. She answered with, "I can, it's a dream come true. I hear you have a new job as well."

In an almost blushing tone he responded, "It's just a little project compared to what you're handling on a daily basis."

She quickly added, "Oh, it's a wonderful opportunity for you, it means the world to Kevin, and I will do anything I can to help." She followed with, "I'm introducing Kevin and Les to Anson tonight."

It took the air out of what had been a friendly conversation until then, and he could not help himself, "Do you think that's a good idea?"

Liz in a sharper tone replied, "He's my fiancé and deserves to know, and besides Kevin has already established some ground rules for tonight."

All he could muster in his response was, "I hope so. It was nice chatting with you." Before hanging up.

Liz thought it was jealously that had prompted his lack of enthusiasm, she knew he still had feelings for her, just as she did him, but it was time to move on.

Chapter 50
Sometimes You Are Right All the Time

The Oxford Hotel is one of the most iconic locations in Denver. Built during one of the early growth phases of Denver in 1891, when you step into the lobby you feel as though you are stepping back into the Gilded Age. The Prohibition era cocktail lounge Cruise Room completes the experience for the first-time guest.

As Kevin and Les approached the lounge he picked up his first Secret Service agent. He had not given it much thought, but any cabinet level position, even the relatively unassuming HHS post, would require a security detail. The addition of these types, while clearly part of the good guy team Kevin had played on, also increased the potential for being recognized as Miles. The members of the detail went into higher alert status as the approached the table.

Anson had noticed a giddiness in his fiancé since they met and hour earlier in his suite. As a male who fed off self confidence in his daily line of work, he had written it off as excitement in seeing him after a couple weeks apart. His charm was still having its desired effect on Liz, and his feelings for her were quite extraordinary...she was an amazing woman. She had announced a surprise for him this evening, which caused his mind to wander in many pleasant directions.

Liz almost jumped out of her chair as Kevin and Les approached, "Here it is Anson, the surprise I told you about. Anson, this is my son Kevin!"

Anson was flabbergasted to say the least and remained in his chair, unable to fully process what Liz had just said. He had heard the stories of Kevin's life from Liz in many scenarios, but the fact he was now a living, breathing human standing in front of him proved overwhelming, even for a man that had experienced the drama of Washington, DC for over 20+ years.

The silence was finally punctuated when Kevin stuck out his hand and announced, "It's a pleasure to meet you Mister Secretary. May I introduce Leslie Richardson."

Anson slowly gathered himself and stood, "Why Kevin, this is an unexpected and wonderful surprise!" In one movement he managed to shake Kevin's hand and usher them to the table to join them. "Please, join us." The table was in a semi-private enclave, so while some other guests had recognized Anson Gamble, and others witnessed the grand entrance of sorts with Kevin and Leslie. The mood in the room quickly returned to its previous calm, and Anson signaled his security detail that everything was OK.

Having returned to their seats, Anson turned to Liz and said, "When were you going to share this little miracle with me?"

Liz gushed, "I just found out this afternoon when Kevin walked into my office. Isn't it wonderful. Now Kevin can give me away at our wedding."

This little detail hit Kevin hard. How had he missed it. He casually glanced at his Mother's left hand, there was no ring. Had he missed another clue? Again, as a former field operative he did not like surprises. Plus, somewhere in his semi-conscious state, he knew the real 'happy ending' he was hoping for was to see his parents reunite with his return. Clearly, it was not to be.

Kevin retorted, "Well, it's good to know we're not the only ones with surprises!"

His Mother almost apologetically, "I'm sorry, it has not been formally announced."

Anson now quickly gathering himself ushered the waiter over to take a drink order, and before anyone else could place their order he proclaimed, "A bottle of your finest champagne! We have reason to celebrate."

Kevin was still learning to be comfortable in his own skin on a general basis, but the added attention was causing him real anxiety. He turned to his mother and in an almost pleading tone asked, "Is there somewhere more private we can continue our catching up with one another?"

His Mother, slightly distracted now with the joy she was feeling looked to Anson, who replied, "We can adjourn to my suite. Waiter, please have the bottle delivered to my room, immediately."

Chapter 51
Paid to Be a Skeptic

In many ways Anson Gamble was paid to be a skeptic, he had heard a number of outlandish stories in his day. As a politician he was an opportunist, and he sensed something yet to be discovered here.

As they settled into the sitting area of the suite, Anson asked the first question, "How did this wonderful news come to be?"

Liz reacting in a most obvious manner, "Don't you see, Kevin was never killed. It was all just a misunderstanding."

Anson smiled as he followed with, "I can see that, but it seems like a little more than a misunderstanding."

Kevin needed to interject quickly, "Yessir, it's quite a bit more. I've shared as much as I can with my folks about the time gap, but am not at liberty to say more at the present time due to matters of national security, etc. I hope you can understand."

To which Anson replied, "I can assure you, when it comes to matters of national security, I am very well versed. Perhaps in some ways, more than you. However, you'll pardon me if I admit that this is a little hard to wrap my head around."

Liz disliked the sudden change in tone and blurted out, "Can't we all just be happy to all be together in this moment?"

Anson not waiting for others to reply spoke first, "I am and will be even happier when I know more of the details. My position in the Cabinet requires it."

Kevin with a serious look directed at Anson, "I can assure you, none of my past ever, and I mean ever, involved HHS. You must accept my word on it."

Anson wasn't backing down, "Mr. Flaherty, my loyalty is to the President of the United States, and he expects me to use my good judgement in all dealings, either personal, public or private. On the surface, it appears to be wonderful news, but there's a great deal left to be filled in to make me comfortable with this recent discovery."

Liz in disbelief, "Anson, this is not all about you. I trust what Kevin has told me, and you must now trust me."

Anson, "Very well, but..."

Kevin stood and reached for Les' hand, "I'm sorry, this was probably too much, too soon for everyone. I should have started my reintroduction more slowly, thoughtfully. We can revisit this more later."

Liz stood, "Where are you going?"

Kevin in a matter-of-fact tone, "Liz and I have some business to resolve in Dallas."

Liz persisted, "And where after that?"

Kevin with a distant look said, "Not sure, I have four families to visit."

The last comment triggered Liz to go to her briefcase and pull out a large folder, "The letters are all here, including postage."

Kevin grabbed the folder and thanked his mother with a hug saying, "We'll be in touch."

His Mother gave him a long knowing look and said, "You better be." She then moved to hug Les and whispered, "Take care of him." To which Les simply nodded.

Kevin turned and shook Anson's hand without a word and he and Les left the suite.

As soon as the door closed, Liz turned to Anson, "We need to talk."

Chapter 52
A Bold Retreat

A s Kevin and Leslie stepped into the brisk evening air Les began the conversation with, "Don't you hate being right all the time?"

Kevin while still processing what had just transpired countered with, "I'd hate to be that guy right now."

Les clarified by asking, "You mean Anson? I'm quite sure he can take care of himself."

To which Kevin replied, "Oh, I'm sure of it, but he's just awakened a mama bear who has not seen her cub for an extended time period and is likely being held accountable for our quick exit from her life again."

Les made an almost yummy sound and while she was already arm in arm with Kevin, she pulled him in closer, "I'm trying to imagine you as a 'cub'." She considered his observation more closely and added, "I see what you mean, I'm sure it's not pretty." Another realization came across her mind, "Hey, for such a tough, alpha dog, you seem to have pretty good instincts on the feminine attitudes."

Kevin smiled and joked, "I always think of myself as the 'chick' in our relationship."

Again, Les pulled him closer, "Well, I wouldn't go that far." Transitioning to a more romantic tone and beginning to feel his strength and courage flooding back into her body and being reminded again of how good he made her feel. "You are sensitive."

His two-word reply, "I'm Irish."

Les purred, "Do you think this Irishman would let me borrow one of his t-shirts tonight?" She knew that image always 'got his motor running'.

To which Kevin replied, "Of course, but I doubt you'll get to wear it very long."

Les in a playful tone, "Are you thinking of getting something started?" Les had a way of acting coy and modest, but inside she loved making love to Kevin as much, if not more than he did. This almost false modesty and coyness was not completely understood by Kevin, but he loved every bit of it, and knew he could never get enough of her.

Kevin replied, "I'm always hoping to get something started, with you." This time he pulled her closer and thought to himself, I am the luckiest guy on the face of the planet...indeed, he was.

In a startled tone Les asked, "Hey, what's in Dallas?"

Kevin said one word, "Closure."

Chapter 53
Her Turn to Be Sorry

An unapologetic Anson Gamble looked over towards his fiancé and spoke flatly, "I'm sure that didn't go as well as you'd hoped?"

Elizabeth was seething inside, but managed to hold it somewhat together, "As well as I'd hoped...? She let the words hang as she struggled to find the right words, "That's almost as bad as 'other than the ending, how did you like the play Mrs. Lincoln'?"

The line brought a slight smile to Anson's lips, and he held out his arm in a gesture intended to pull Liz in towards him. He was used to his charm working for him in these situations. In both his public and personal life, it had been the more difficult situations that had allowed him to advance his political career. It would fail him this time.

An unrelenting Liz practically recoiled from the gesture an offered, "It was not intended to be funny."

Anson absorbed the verbal blow and sensed he had really stepped in it now. It was his experience that now told him he need to shut up and just take what was coming, let the other party rant or punch itself out, much as Muhammad Ali had done with boxer George Foreman in his famous 'rope a dope strategy'. It was not lost on Anson, that this strategy, along with many other that had led the champ to be stricken with Parkinson's Disease. He would not allow himself to be hit as hard for as long. He dropped his arms slowly from their welcoming pose to a more neutral, almost surrendering gesture.

It was Liz's turn to pile on, "You drove away the son I had lost for a lifetime?" She began showing emotional signs in her voice and gestures.

Anson knew better, it was as though Ali came out of the strategy too soon and Foreman still had his lethal punch, "Well, I don't know...?"

Liz put her hand up in the shape of a stop sign, "Oh yes you do." The words landed like a right cross to the jaw. Liz followed with, "I've never seen you unable to adapt to a scene, especially one that had the potential for such joy. I was being awakened from a long nightmare of having lost my only child. A son who acted heroically on behalf of his Country and brothers in arms. A son who had the brightest of futures in his young life."

Anson, now shaking his head in a sign of agreement took a step forward Liz, this time even more sternly put up the stop sign.

Liz dropped he hand down but continued to shake her head emphatically, "No...no, this had the potential for being the happiest day of my life. I was going to share the best news I could ever receive with the man I'd loved, but it was taken from me with your selfish and uncaring actions. I really don't want to say what I am thinking right now." Her shoulders slumped and she began to softly sob.

Anson heard the past tense around the word 'love'. He reviewed his personal 'playbook' from past altercations but had nothing that resembled that even remotely resembled this scenario. He prepared to speak the truth, even though it felt completely awkward for him, "You think I'm jealous?"

It was Liz's turn to absorb words from another, she nodded yes, and a slight shudder ran through her body. She knew what she was preparing to do and felt 100% entitled and empowered. She was breaking off her engagement from a man she thought she had loved. An ambitious and somewhat powerful man, politically speaking, who might someday be President. There was no other course she could take...she loved her newfound son more than life itself, and Anson had displayed a character flaw she could not accept.

Anson attempted to fight back, but his verbal jab only found air and made matters much worse with, "You can't walk out on me? Think what the media will do with this story?" The words hung momentarily, and he wished he could suck them back into his mouth. He might as well have said, "You know you're right about me, and just to reinforce it let me shoot myself in the foot."

Liz turned a picked up her purse. All she could manage as she stepped out the door was, "I'm sorry Anson."

As soon as the door closed, he called his Chief of Staff and without introduction said, "I need you to find everything you can about Kevin Flaherty. Yes, that Kevin Flaherty. Yes, everything!"

Liz managed to make it to the lobby before dialing the number. The voice at the other end of the phone questioned, "Liz?"

She sputtered, "He tried to take him away from me again."

The other voice replied, "Well, we'll never, ever let that happen." They were the exact words at the exact time she needed to hear at that moment. He always knew how to comfort her when she needed it the most...it was Kevin's father.

Chapter 54
Final Closure

The next day in Dallas, Rosie was again ushered into the Conference Room. Special Agent Withers stood by the door and was soon joined by Special Agent Walker.

Walker shared the results from the Alamo, including the capture of El Patron. It had been entirely successful, and he added that it would be included in whatever sentencing was levied against him in the form of leniency, although he wasn't exactly sure what that meant.

For a moment Rosie almost felt like he was back on the team, before reminding himself that could never happen.

Walker stood up and made a half turn towards the door, "Oh, by the way, there's someone else who'd like to see you." He stepped out and took both of Leslie's hands into his, "You sure you got this?"

Leslie nodded, "In Sam's and Miles names, I got this." Walker ushered her in. Kevin had needed to set this up in her behalf, but he couldn't be near the facility. They had both learned the hard way that secrets were best left alone, and someone from either side recognizing him at this point could undo the noble work of Daf and others. In other words, this was her walk to take alone.

As soon as she'd left him the phone rang, it was his father telling him his mother had broken off her engagement with Anson and was now on her way to Florida...he sounded hopeful. Kevin told his father he and Leslie would grab a flight to Florida on their way to vacation. His father said that would be great and asked where they were going. Kevin replied, Ireland.

Back in the Conference Room Leslie walked in and took a seat across the table from Rosie. The expression on Rosie's face reminded Special Agent Withers of the line from his favorite film Tombstone. In it, Doc Holiday says to a surprised gunfighter he's about ready to discharge, "Why Johnny Ringo, you look like someone just walked over your grave." It was effective in the film, just as Les' mere presence was in this room.

Finally, a clearly troubled Rosie broke the silence with, "Look, I'm sorry they were both good men, and I screwed it all up. I don't know what else I can do or say."

An unflinching Leslie gathered herself and never leaving here glare from Rosie delivered, "No, you're wrong they were great men. They served their country and their brothers in arms honorably...something you'd know nothing about." At this point she dropped her head downward and in a halting manner said, "And I loved them both."

The final line caught everyone a bit off guard, but they would not question it, and presumed she meant in diverse ways. It was intentional and she thought it would help cover the trail for Kevin's past lives.

She closed with, "I don't know what your future is, but I hope you can manage to bring something good from it, whatever that is...I intend to honor both in the best way I know how, in service," It almost sounded like forgiveness, but then she added, "But you tried to remove all happiness from my life, and I will not give you that satisfaction. I am neither a victim or a survivor, I am just me, and I choose to be happy and live a good life."

Everyone in that room took something different from her words, but they were all powerful in their own way. She was taking control of her own life, her destiny, as only everyone can.

By the time she made it back to Kevin she literally fell into his arms. She looked up into his hazel eyes and said, "Thank you, I needed that." For the first time she realized they were the same color as Sam's, how fitting.

Kevin, now taking after his father smiled and said merely, "No, we needed that."

Leslie smiled and said, "Where to next?"

Kevin looking outward, as if he was trying to find his future said, "We have a quick stop in Florida we need to make, and then I have a cottage rented outside Dublin for a month or longer."

Leslie smiled that naughty little smile of hers and said, "I think I have a little Irish in me."

Part 2 - The Best Man

Chapter 1

"God Invented Whisky to Keep the Irish from Ruling the World!"
Anonymous

Kevin pondered the quote as he sat at the bar at his favorite pub. He had discovered The Brazen in his third week in Ireland. It was the oldest pub in Ireland, founded in 1138, and was the least likely to have a large influence of tourists of all the pubs in the Temple Bar district. He had also come to enjoy the wisdom of the bartenders there.

As Kevin took his first pull of the afternoon of the most famous Irish export, Guiness, he mused on it being more of a meal than a beer. He had never reviewed the nutritional elements of the dark and robust stout, why should he, it would likely ruin the illusion, and there was certainly no reason for that.

Kevin caught his favorite bartender, Seamus (the Irish equivalent of James with roots in Latin and Hebrew) during a lull in the late afternoon and posed a question he had been pondering for quite some time:

Kevin posed the question, "Seamus, do you know the difference between Dublin and London?"

Seamus in a brisk manner responded, "Tell me." Many would have seen the shortness of a response such as this as a sign of indifference, but in this case, it meant he was truly anxious to hear the "difference" between the two and did not want to waste any time getting there.

Kevin studies the contents of his pint glass and mused, "In London the statues are of monarchs and military leaders, and in Dublin they are all of poets."

The words floated across the bar and were absorbed by Seamus who muttered the single word, "Brilliant!" This constituted high praise from him, and Kevin felt a bit profound for the moment.

During his month in Ireland Kevin had felt a multitude of emotions...a rekindling of his ancestral roots, the beauty of getting to know people on a truly personal level and the opportunity to ponder and subject that interested him. No longer was he a slave to the 'mission'. It had also allowed him to fall even more deeply in love with Leslie. Gone were the dramatic moments when their lives seemed at risk at every turn.

Seamus followed his latest response with, "Where's the missus?" He knew the two were not married and had frequently advised Kevin to 'put a ring on it'. He was quite fond of Leslie, as most men were, with her ability to hang with the men during a round of darts while holding a full pint. She could be 'one of the boys' but was clearly a fine lady.

It was Kevin's turn to respond, and he ignored the 'missus' comment, "Showing my parents around, my father wanted to see Trinity University." Trinity was a special place with many famed alumni, including James Joyce, Oscar Wilde, Samuel Beckett to name a few. His father's love of academia had drawn him to it. In a typical knock against the Irish, it was ranked the 101st university in the world...it just could not be in the Top 100.

To which Seamus replied, "Ah, playing the tourist are they?" Kevin found most of the Irish liked if not loved Yanks. The connection was largely due to their common struggle with the Brits and the legacy of those of Irish descent who had risen in its highest echelons...this stopping and starting with John F. Kennedy. Oddly enough, they were also enamored with Bill Clinton, and Kevin thought it must have something to do with his 'human weaknesses.'

One of the best residual outcomes of Kevin's reintroduction to the land of the living was the reconnecting of his parents. His alleged death had pushed them apart, but they had never really stopped loving one another. Their current status and arrival in Dublin had brought both Kevin and Leslie additional joy.

As if directed on a film version of this life, the door opened and in walked Les, Elizabeth and Jim. They all seemed to be happier than ever. Kevin thought to himself, Les has that effect on people. As Kevin motioned to Seamus for a round for his family he commented, "You all seem happy. Did you like seeing the university?"

Elizabeth and Jim gushed, "We loved it, especially the..."

Kevin, not letting the words to tail off to far responded, "Especially what?"

Liz looked over at Jim who nodded in the affirmative, "Especially the chapel." The Parker Chapel is named after Margarite B. Parker, the wife of George Parker, a petroleum pioneer who died in 1965 before the chapel was finished. It is located on the western edge of campus. Liz continued her statement with, "We've chosen it as where your father and I can restate our vows. We met with the minister, and he agreed to conduct the ceremony." Having been technically divorced and not willing to annul their original marriage, Kevin would be seen as a bastard in the eyes of many within the Catholic Church.

Jim continued with, "We didn't want to say anything until we knew it could be done, and you want to hear the best news?"

It was Kevin's turn, "Tell me."

Jim and Liz in unison, "You get to be the best man!"

Les immediately followed with, "and I'm the Maid of Honor!"

Kevin was beaming with pride and a moment of sheer joy in hearing the good news...what could possibly go wrong.

Chapter 2
Anger is Like Malaria, it Never Truly Goes Away

Meanwhile back in the States an ever-growing ambition and bitterness fueled the actions of one Anson Gamble. The breakup with Elizabeth was festering with his image of himself. Woman do not break-off engagements with him, he breaks them off, in typically hurtful manners, with them. He imagined winning Liz back after she came to her senses and then "kicking her to the curb."

Of course, none of this would ever happen in real life, and only served to illustrate his own insecurities or worse. The only relationships he had ever managed to sustain were due to his status, and not any particular qualities that drew woman to him. He was not forthright in sharing his feelings demonstrating affection.

He typically preyed on younger women with some lack of confidence. Of course, Liz was not one of these women. She was very sure of herself and had always put family first, even during the dark period where she had nearly given up on her son. His actions during the return of what she held most dear had finished him in her eyes now and forever. There was positively no opportunity to redeem his image in any way, shape or form.

But why then had Anson deviated so far off his normal path in finding a partner. Once again, his ambition had gotten the best of him. He had imagined Liz on his arm during a presidential campaign. She was made for being a supportive spouse...strong, smart, attractive, eloquent and empathetic. Many of the qualities Anson did not share. Her rise from being a volunteer to the upper echelons of VA leadership played extremely well. Public health remained a key topic in any election and the military post-Vietnam had regained some of its support among voters.

Anson needed to be patient, which was another quality he lacked. He was more in step with the cartoon character, Wiley E. Coyote...a diabolical genius. He had been lampooned throughout his life in this political career in such a way. He would misstep in his efforts to recover Liz, but the frustration would cause him to act out in the worst conceivable way. Time would indeed tell.

Chapter 3
How Did you Know?

The celebration in Dublin was muted. While Kevin and Liz had been embraced by the locals, they did not have a large volume of friends, and Jim and Liz had only arrived a week earlier.

When they left The Brazen and strolled to their updated cottage a half mile or so from the Temple Bar District there was an aura of joy that could not be diminished. As far as Kevin was concerned, his return had gone even better than he had hoped it would. The meeting with Anson the only blemish and moving forward he saw no reason to look in the rear-view mirror.

He and his father stepped outside with a cigar and a full two finger of 18-year-old Jameson whisky. The bottle would sell for $150 or more in the US, but the absence of tariffs and taxes brought the local cost down quite a bit, and as they say... 'when in Dublin'. The Irish were social drinkers, in fact those who drank at home privately were viewed suspiciously. This however was a special night.

The ladies would join them shortly. Leslie would sit as close to Kevin as possible. The cigar smoke did not bother her, and she was likely to take a few puffs and sip with Kevin whatever was in his glass. Kevin cherished these moments and would never grow tired of them.

His mother on the other hand would give them both the 'stink eye' and plainly state that she had not suffered all these years to lose her son to cancer. Kevin would respect her wishes once she arrived outside at the peat burning fire pit. He had asked Les to keep his mom inside for a few minutes, he had to ask his father an important question.

After a quick toast, Kevin's favorite, "May you arrive in heaven a half hour before the devil knows you're dead." Kevin looked in all seriousness at his father and asked, "How did you know?"

A perplexed Jim Flaherty answered with, "How did I know what?"

Kevin shook his head in realizing he had not been very clear gathered his thoughts and after another tug at his cigar and sip of the smooth Irish elixir restated, "Mom, that she was the one?"

Now it was the father's turn to take pulls from both his cigar and whisky glass, "Gosh Kevin, there were so many things. She was/is beautiful, confident, fun and as you well know loyal." Jim let the words sit there as he smiled and added, "Oh, and one other thing...I could not imagine living without her!"

Kevin simply nodded.

Jim followed up with his own question, "Why do you ask?" Knowing full well why his son had tendered the question.

Kevin looked up into the starry night and offered a simple, "Just trying to sort things out."

Jim in his best college professor tone, "Well I wouldn't sort too long, she's terrific!"

It was Kevin's turn to smile, "I know. I've never felt this way. I never even dreamed I would feel this way about another person. The thing is, I guess what I'm really trying to say is we've been through a lot. She was recently widowed and all..."

Jim getting even more serious, "Kevin, life can be uncertain. You know that better than most. You've been given a 'do over' of sorts, and the only other thing you'll ever regret is losing her, trust me."

Kevin nodded more forcibly. The 'do over' comment reminded him of Daf. He had said the same thing, and the fact his father had used the same words reinforced the message. All Kevin could muster was, "Thanks Dad." His father didn't know, and hopefully would never know the other critical component in he and Les being together, no nightmares.

Jim decided to go looking for his reincarnated bride-to-be and said simply, "I'll leave you with your thoughts."

Kevin knew now what he needed to do. His mind drifted off in several directions unrelated to his romantic opportunity:

- The fundraising for the foundation was off to a great start.
- Most of the recipients of the initial letter had contributed the most they could, and better yet, they all vowed to create local fundraising efforts.

- They needed to begin finding other non-family board members.
- And most importantly, Kevin needed to visit four families. His own closure.

Just then the love of his life popped out onto the outside seating area and slid into his lap. As expected, she borrowed his cigar and took a few puffs. It was long thought that it was unfeminine for women to smoke cigars, and while Les took a few obligatory puffs, she wasn't truly 'smoking' a cigar. She handed it back and reached for his glass. As she breathed in the wonderful scent of the Jameson, honey colored with hints of tropical fruit, caramel and nutmeg, and slowly raised it to her lips she inquired, "A penny for your thoughts?"

Kevin rearranged her position on his lap and clearly stated, "There worth a lot more than that."

Les shrugged and said, "Then at least tell me about what you were thinking."

Kevin pondered the question and held his glass up towards the nearly full moon, "The future. How do you like that?"

Again, Les reached over and intercepted the glass, took a sip and placed it on the ground, and as only she could do, placed her hands on both sides of his face and planted a slow, soft kiss on Kevin's lips. They both had cigar and whisky breath, so neither seemed to mind. She pulled back slowly and gave Kevin a look that went right to his very soul, "Oh, I love the future. As long as I am in it."

Kevin in absorbing the entire moment caressed the side of her face and whispered, "There is no other."

A contented Leslie draped her arms around him and let her head fall onto his chest. It was her happy place.

Chapter 4
Character Does Count

Whaat motivates people? There were many views on this concept: love, power, money, status and other principles. Maslow would suggest the following in his Hierarchy of Needs:

- Physiological needs - air, water, food, etc.
- Safety needs - personal security, employment, resources, etc.
- Love and belonging - friendship, intimacy, sense of connection, etc.
- Esteem - respect, self-esteem, status, etc.
- Self-actualization - the desire to become the most one could be.

In assessing Anson against these criteria, you would expect he would rank highly in most of them. On a personal level he never had been self-aware of his own strengths and weaknesses, never recognized there was a better person within his own being and most importantly did not care. Even his self-described mentors were slow to recognize his true character flaws, and only saw what he was willing to show them.

Dwight Eisenhower, the acclaimed Supreme Allied Commander of Allied Forces in WWII and 34th President of the United States once observed Richard M. Nixon, his own Vice President and future 37th President, "I never knew a man that did not have one true friend." The same could be said for Anson. Friends were tools to be used as needed. Many people began relationships with him only to discover the truth the hard way.

Were these people naive or duped into thinking that Anson's motives were as pure as he portrayed them to be? The reality was most saw only sound bites, whether on the CNN broadcasts or even face-to-face, Anson was measured and guarded, you only saw what he wanted you to see.

American's love all the true character of a leader...honesty, strength, empathy and even courage amid a crisis. It's what allowed us to celebrate true leaders and hastened the demise of those who could only pretended to achieve this status. Most leaders, whether real or presumed, would be tested and either gain higher status or be sent to the "junk pile" of human history. Anson did not realize he was creating his own "test" and that it would in turn hasten his own status in the rough and tumble world of national politics and leadership.

Unbeknownst to Anson was the role his ex-fiancé's son had played in what had led to what was becoming known as the 2nd Victory at the Alamo. The first had gained independence and ultimately US statehood for Texas, and the 2nd was a clear victory in the US campaign against the most powerful Mexican cartel. It was hard to determine just how much of a win it would be for the current administration, El Patron was fully engaged in cooperating with the Feds, led by the efforts of Special Agent Walker, but it seemed as though it may quickly become what was needed to stem the tide of the poison being imported across our borders.

Anson recognized it was a train he needed to be on, and if he was brought on board quickly enough, he could convince future voters he had something to do with it. The challenge would be getting on board a train that had already left the station.

Chapter 5
Who Am I

Back in Ireland, and while Anson was falling short in his self-actualization process, Kevin was plotting his own course in warp speed.

In his new role he could nor just be accountable for himself and the mission, there were individuals like Les and his parents, along with others, who would come to rely upon him in a variety of roles. In some ways it terrified him.

He recalled a friend once saying that his ex-wife was "to needy" and he did not want to be "needed." They both had laughed at the 'punchline', and now Kevin was beginning to feel needed. It made him feel good. as he was learning many feelings did, but they carried responsibilities as well.

By any measure Kevin was a hero. He had acted in many a heroic fashion after another, but could you consider him a true "American" hero? Kevin contemplated this perspective more fully with the following thoughts:

• In the war he was fighting for his team members and the pilots he needed to rescue. He had no issues with the enemy other than the harm they were trying to inflict upon his guys. They were no true threat to America.

• As an operative he viewed his actions as a struggle of good versus evil. There were overlaps between this struggle an US interest, but most of his efforts were targeted against enemies who were bad people period.

• His efforts against the cartel were the closest to an act of American heroism, and the killing of Sam and efforts to do the same to he and Les made it personal, but the cartel was a for-profit entity. While they brought harm to the citizens of the US, they were not intent to destroying it. We were simply a market for the poison they were selling.

In absorbing all these factors Kevin knew his journey of self-discovery required needed to take several paths:

He needed to visit the four families of the pilots he could not save. He knew

1.   There was something out there that would bring closure to the life he had lived up until now.

2.   His instincts told him there was one battle left to fight. He did not know where or when, but he knew it was out there.

3.   And most importantly, he desperately wanted to become the man Les wanted him to be.

As Kevin prepared for their return. He was a man of action, not of words preparing for action and as Ben Franklin once said, "Well done is better than well said."

Chapter 6
Discovery

Kevin had needed Ireland. It gave him a powerful sense of who he was and where he had come from...roots as it were. He was no longer the cold, efficient operative he had trained and performed for all those years. He was changing emotionally, physically, and even spiritually. When he looked in the mirror, he was beginning to like what he saw more and more.

As it was important for Kevin, it was even more so for Leslie. Not for her own personal discovery, but in watching Kevin evolve into the man he was meant to be...his own best man.

The Kevin she knew in high school was full of hope. She had witnessed a sharp, dramatic change into the Miles and Jake versions she met in Spain. Kevin had become the tough, calculating and effective agent that fought the good fight in many arenas. This man had saved her life both literally and figuratively. She would always be grateful to him and had fallen in love with him in a passionate and dramatic fashion, but she liked this version even more.

She saw how he loved his reunited parents. How he engaged with others, demonstrated kindness to complete strangers in a pure and intentional manner...oh, and the 'twinkle in his eyes'. The playfulness of a grown man in situations that were new to him. He had never been in love before, and he loved her in a fierce yet gentle way she could not fully describe and never wanted to lose.

His parents' renewal of their vows was a quaint and quite aware in the Chapel at Trinity University. Both Kevin and Leslie wished silently wished it was the two of them standing at that alter. Kevin had considered making it a 'two-fer' and marry Les there as well but thought better of it. His parents deserved this time as their own.

Rather than return to the cottage that night Kevin got his parents a room at the Shelbourne. One of the oldest hotels in Dublin, opened in 1824, it is rich in its history and carries an elegant demeanor for all guests...especially those on their 2nd honeymoon.

It allowed Kevin and Leslie to chat about their return to the states. Kevin needed to visit the four families from his list. He had crafted follow-up letters to each of them announcing his upcoming personal visit. Each family, such as they were, he allowed to opt out of his visit if they felt it would be too difficult or reopen old scars. None had opted out.

Leslie desperately wanted to join him. She knew how difficult it would be for him, confronting this part of his past, and the nightmares he had been able to suppress...they would never fully go away. Kevin insisted he take this journey alone. A frustrated Leslie insisted they fly together from Dublin back to the US before temporarily going their separate ways. She had some of her own past to deal with in closing out her life with Sam.

The next few days Kevin said his 'goodbyes' to Dublin. He knew a part of him would always be there and promised himself and others he would return. As he shook the hand of his favorite bar tender Seamus he heard, "I shall miss you Kevin Flaherty!" Kevin reflected on a life in which he had never heard those words spoken. He liked it and hoped he would hear them again.

Chapter 7

"He That Lies Down with Dogs, Wakes up With Fleas," Ben Franklin or "Never Take Credit Where Credit is Not Due," Special Agent Walker

In DC Anson met with Bryce the following morning. Of course, there had been no call from the President, and the meeting with the two FBI agents had not gone well. Neither appeared to be impressed with the trapping of the Secretary's office or personal status, and both would require some "active management" by he and Bryce.

Anson began with the following directive, "Get out to all your contacts within the task force and let them know in was our intent to have Withers be the primary liaison. We do not want Walker appearing to have any strength in deciding who or what is happening here." Anson thought to himself...we will teach the bastard what hard knuckle politics feels like.

Bryce made a note of what he was asked to do but could not help but wonder...are not we all on the same team. He had occasionally had these thoughts in the past, but now his boss's rants were directed towards the FBI, not someone you wanted to pick a fight within DC.

Next Anson asked for what Bryce had uncovered regarding Kevin Flaherty. Bryce reported, "Pretty much as we were told. He was reported KIA approximately 15-16 years ago and was awarded the Medal of Honor posthumously. He was renowned in the heroic actions he took in recovering downed pilots in enemy territory. A real hero." Bryce did not fully understand the axe he had to grind with Kevin and his ex-fiancé.

Anson clearly disappointed stammered, "That's all?"

Bryce, "Yessir."

Anson becoming more agitated, "OK, you contact your new BFF and ask him what he knows about Kevin Flaherty."

Bryce thinking more clearly asked, "What if he asks why we want it?"

A now perturbed Anson gushed, "I don't care. Think of something. If not, just play the national security card."

Bryce mused to himself, "Let's see, The Secretary of Health & Human Services' Chief of Staff wants to know the background of a true American hero for national security reasons. The whole idea felt laughable." He was worried about his boss.

Chapter 8
(2 + 2 = 6)

Later the next day Walker had an update call with Special Agent Withers. The primary topic was again the "task force" and Walker was concerned with a multitude of issues:

- Will it limit their effectiveness?
- Will it slow them down?
- Will it compromise their stealth in pursuing the target?
- Will it put his team at any greater risk?

The last two points were of the greatest concern, or so it seemed, politicians love to take credit for positive results, whether they should take credit is entirely beside the point. Walker was quite good at sharing credit with others for the following reasons: 1) he did not need or want the attention himself, and 2) if directed toward others it could create motivation for others to help him with other cases. However, he did have a problem with others accepting credit where it was not deserved, and he knew this would be the case with Gamble.

Towards the end of their call Withers brought forward an additional comment that was not on the Agenda, His new BFF had called and wanted to know about a Kevin Flaherty. The name did not ring a bell for either man, and Bryce was not able to share where their interest in the individual stemmed from...national security and all that nonsense.

Withers had done a quick name search and found an individual by the same name who had been KIA during the war in Southeast Asia. In digesting the information Walker muttered, "Poor son-of-a-bitch!"

Withers shared one additional comment, "He was awarded the Medal of Honor posthumously."

This got Walker's full attention from a respect and admiration perspective. He followed with, "Anything else?"

Withers announced, "One more thing. His mother was a high-level director with the Veteran's Administration who just resigned."

Walker again, "Anything else?"

Withers chimed, "No sir, not yet."

Walker ended the call with, "OK, I'll handle this inquiry from here on out and let you know what I find out. If Bryce or Anson, ask any more questions refer them to me." Walker's instincts were telling him there was more to this casual inquiry than met the eye, and he wanted to find out first who this individual was or is before Gamble did.

Withers only additional comment was, "Gladly"

Walker made two calls relating to Kevin Flaherty in the next 30 minutes. Who is this guy?

Chapter 9
Back Home

As the Flaherty clan arrived back in the states, their first stop was in Atlanta, and they were all heading in different directions.

Liz and Jim back to Gainesville and their renewed life together, including the Foundation they were now jointly running. The two of them would be a dynamic pair, and Daf's legacy was in good hands.

Les reluctantly headed to Dallas to 'clean-up some issues pertaining to Sam, without Kevin. She did not like being apart from him ever and knew the journey he was on could bring back some old 'demons'.

Kevin's return and planned trip was unsettling. He was still not completely comfortable in his home country, having spent most of his adult life abroad, and the four planned meetings, while difficult to choreograph and even harder to set expectations on, were all that was left in completing his 'list'. He had lived with it for so long it was hard to imagine not having it in the forethought of his daily living. He knew it would be good for him on a personal level to bring closure and hoped the same were true for his audience.

Les made one more desperate plea to 'tag along'. She was clearly worried about the impact of the meetings on him, but deep inside she knew how much she would miss him as well...she loved the entire man, strengths as well as weaknesses, they all made up the entire package.

She clutched his arm and began with, "I promise I'll be good company."

Kevin knew in his heart there were no truer words that could be spoken, "I know, this is something I need to do alone."

Les in a pouting manner, "You don't like me anymore?"

They both knew that was not the case. Kevin could not imagine loving anyone more. He responded with, "You know that's not true."

Les somewhat sheepishly, "I do." and continued with, "But if you need me, all you have to do is call, OK?"

Kevin nodded and after a long embrace they headed their separate ways. As Les strolled through her gate she remembered the night in Madrid, and how she had worried so much about him after the two Marines from the embassy had inadvertently brought up tough memories for him. That night had ended as the most intimate and special moments of their joint lives together, but this time she would not be there. The thought of not being there was almost more than she could bear.

Just then her cell phone rang, and a voice said, 'I need you." It was Kevin.

She gushed, "I'll be right there."

Kevin responded, "Not necessary, I just wanted to make sure it worked. I have my big boy pants on."

Now in a lighter mood she replied, "Well, you better make sure you keep them on, Buster." It was a thinly veiled suggestion he could not think about receiving comfort from anyone else.

Kevin could not even imagine being with anyone else and ended the call with a straightforward, "Love you with all my heart." She knew he did, and right now that was all that mattered in her world.

As always, Les responded with, "I do too. See you in Gainesville." The call ended and her heart sank a little. Kevin always told her she could do anything, and in most situations, he was right...except for the thought of losing him.

Chapter 10
Investigation/Putting the Puzzle Together

The two calls Special Agent Walker made to contacts within the State Department and veteran's Administration. They were for to people he trusted and more importantly, people who trusted him. The plot was about to become thicker in a hurry.

The VA call was simpler but carried with it strong implications on what was happening regarding Kevin Flaherty in this case. Yes, she was a high-ranking leader with a bright future who had abruptly resigned his contact began. There was a rumor someone had recently come back into her life or risen from the dead. Walker wondered if that could be Kevin. It seemed farfetched...that was for Lazarus only, right?

At the end of the call his contact blurted out, "One more thing, she just ended her engagement too. Walker being a thorough investigator, but doubting it had any basis on his situation inquired, "Do we know with whom?"

His VA contact, "Some sleazy politician, Anson Gamble."

Walker without demonstrating any emotion that could have fed his contacts curiosity simply responded, "Thank you."

Walker thought to himself, why that 'sleazebag', using the FBI to investigate the personal life of his ex-fiancé. He made note of it and moved on. Nothing done by an egocentric politician surprised him anymore, and when you add love to any scenario it stirred things up.

The call to the State Department was more complex but added more seriousness to the topic. His contact had initially come to a dead end in their inquiries, but then someone recalled a story coming out of Madrid, although they were not sure of the details.

Fortunately, Walker had a contact in the US embassy in Madrid, a fraternity brother named John Arnold who was the Chief of Staff for the Ambassador. Initially, John was reluctant to share anything with Walker...all this 'need to know' policy, but then realized it was official FBI business. Plus, he knew he could trust Walker.

An operative by the name of Jake Gallagher had come into the embassy a couple of months ago. They had been authorized from the highest authority, including the President to cooperate with him on whatever he needed. One of his requests had been to reestablish his original identity, Kevin Flaherty. The embassy complied, picked up the tab for few nights in Madrid for him and his travel companion and made their travel arrangements. Walker asked where they were headed and Arnold responded, "Florida, I think."

He asked one final question, "Do you recall his travel companion's name?"

Arnold responded, "Yes, very well, she was 'easy on the eyes'... Leslie Grant. We changed her identity too. She went back to her maiden name."

Multiple alarms were now going off in Walker's head. This was becoming very interesting. Sam Grant's widow was now with Kevin Flaherty, an ex-marine who was allegedly KIA many years ago, and of personal interest to Anson Gamble. This could be fun.

Chapter 11
Making it Personal

Meanwhile, Anson was beside himself with the lack of information being provided through his Chief of Staff, Bryce and his other sources. His rage in being rejected by Kevin's mother was made even more lethal due to his intention that somehow all this might bring Elizabeth Flaherty back to him. It would lead to his undoing.

In all interactions with Bryce now the intelligence gathering on Kevin Flaherty took priority against all real work the Secretary of HHS should be conducting. The other staff members were noticing his behavior as well, and some of them were now approaching Bryce and wondering what was wrong?

These inquiries, along with his own concerns, drove Bryce to the following exchange at the start of their next 1:1 meeting...

Anson began with, "Where are we on the Flaherty investigation?"

A frustrated Bryce, "Is that what we're calling it now?"

Anson in a somewhat coy response, "Well, of course. What else would you call it?"

Bryce curtly, "A casual inquiry on a coincidental meeting."

Anson now more agitated, "You can be assured it is much more than that..."

Bryce realizing, he needed to avert his boss from making a mistake that could influence his career as well as Bryce's, "Sir, Mr. Secretary. I really do not know what else to call it. I do not see how this ends favorably for us, and at the minimum we're wasting resources on the important work that needs to be done by our department."

A now indignant Anson, "Wasting resources? Our department? I'll remind you this is my department."

Bryce taking a step back, but not willing to surrender the field entirely, "Then how does the "Flaherty investigation fit into our work being done here?"

Anson seeming to gather himself, "It's a clear issue of 'national security'."

Bryce in a measured tone, "Alright, then should it not be assigned to Homeland Security or the Justice Department?"

Anson began recognizing the logic in his Chief of Staff's questioning, and while he was beginning to understand his concerns, he was not prepared to abandon his pursuit, "OK, from this point forward I'll take lead on it."

This newly directed course bothered Bryce even more than the previous one. He could now not keep track of the Secretary's actions and decided on a more diplomatic approach, "Mr. Secretary, you certainly have more critical issues that would require your attention?"

Anson now growing tired of the 'interrogation' he was being given by his subordinate declared, "That will be all."

The abruptness of the meeting being ended, and his dismissal created even greater warning lights for Bryce. He had seen signs of this petty behavior in the past. In one case it had led to an act of recrimination by his boss, then Senator that concerned him to this day. This time the stage was larger, and the penalties could be even more severe. Bryce's only response was, "Yessir." but there was clearly more work to be done to avoid his be hit with shrapnel from Anson's blunder into a league he was not ready to play in.

Chapter 12
Making Use of One's Assets

With his newfound data on Kevin Flaherty, including the linkage to Leslie Grant, now Leslie Richardson, not quite fitting together, Walker decided to visit another source to confirm his instincts. He walked into the familiar conference room and there sat Roosevelt.

The last time Walker had been in the room Leslie Grant had administered a surgical strike of emotions on the loss of two brave men at the hands of Rosie, her husband Sam, and Miles Fender. During her delivery she had said something that still intrigued Walker, "I loved both of them."

It had not meant to much at the time, it was the combining of two American heroes, but was beginning to concern Walker more and more. Walker began the meeting with a casual, "Rosie, how are they treating you?" This was the best Walker could muster. In his eyes, no matter how much he cooperated with the authorities, was a traitor to his country and had betrayed two brothers in the law enforcement domain.

Rosie responded, "Not bad, I guess as well as I deserve. What can I help you with today?"

Walker ignored the opening remark, he really did not care, but followed with, "We're trying to connect the dots on the close of our operation at the Alamo."

Rosie responded, "Gothcha."

Walker continued, "In your dealings with Miles Fender did you ever run into the name Jake Gallagher?"

Rosie smiling responded, "You're kidding right."

Walker in a measured tone, "Rosie, you know I never kid about these types of issues."

Rosie pulling back on his giddiness, "OK, I'm sorry. I just thought you had to know. Miles assumed the identity Jake Gallagher in his retirement from being an operative."

Walker took a minute to get his head around that piece of information, that would mean Miles became Jake and Jake became the reborn Kevin.

The look on his face prompted Rosie to add, "After the career Miles had, there were a lot of enemies who would do him harm, so they must be given new identities."

Certainly, Walker could appreciate the needs for an identity change in this line of work, but there were two questions that remained unanswered, "I thought Miles was killed in that gunfight in Valencia?"

Rosie nodded, "So did everyone else. My guess is a third party was used as a dead Miles to seal the lid on Miles's existence. The cartel, or anyone else, do not have time to chase dead people, right?"

Rather than ask the obvious question of who was used in Mike place, which Rosie would not have known the answer to, Walker said in a question to himself, "Well, then how did Leslie fit into all this?"

Rosie offered, "Sam and Miles were partners and trusted one another." The word 'trust' seemed out of place coming from Rosie's mouth. "Sam had instructed Leslie that if things went down bad, really bad, she should contact Miles. Kind of a last-ditch source of protection. Miles had already become Jake by the time Leslie needed his help."

Once again, Walker needed a moment to "fill in the dots" but was beginning to understand how one man had been played the role of three in this scenario...man, he must be good. Maybe the best.

Chapter 13
Making A List, Checking It Twice

A s Kevin headed into the "home stretch" of finishing his personal journey with his list, he had a combination of emotions fueling this final phase:

- How would he be received?
- Would it help the recipients of his visit find closure in their lives?
- What would be the lessons learned in the overall process?
- Would it create additional connections that could help support the Foundation.

While Miles had developed a hard cover of cynicism in his previous role, and Jake had helped him bring back a sense of romanticism in what could be, it was his true self, Kevin who was beginning to see the inherent good in people. It was captivating for him to know this about his new world.

This 'barnstorming' tour would take a total of four days, two for travel and two intense meeting days of meeting with the contacts he had made via the letters of introduction. It was fortuitous that there were two clusters of the four-meeting located near one another.

The first two were located outside of Kansas City. Both of these men had been single at the time of their death, Lt. Timothy "the Dagger" Daggett and Lt. Charles "Ground Chuck" Strassel. Lt. Daggett had been flying an F4 Phantom in support of a raid into the north and was taken down by a surface to air missile. Lt. Strassel as his nickname would suggest was flying close air to ground support in an A6 Intruder. He had been a hero himself for his efforts to support his fellow Marines on the ground and had been a little too zealous in his last mission. He was taken down by a variety of close-range ground fire, including a lucky shot into the heavily armored cockpit.

The parents of both men fully appreciated the efforts of Kevin coming to visit and asked what they could do to thank him...he referenced the Foundation, and they both quickly sent a generous donation and promised it would not be their last.

Satisfied that both meetings had gone as well as could be expected, Kevin caught a 'red eye' to San Diego, CA. This was done for two reasons, he had a full day tomorrow in Southern California, and the 'red eye' prevented him from sleeping and the potential for the nightmares to return.

In route he phoned Leslie and shared the results of his first two meetings. She was delighted to hear from him, missed him terribly and looked forward to reconnecting back in Florida. She knew how important this was for him and secretly wished for the day they could leave it behind and focus on their new life together...if that were possible.

She said she loved him with all her heart and said goodbye. For obvious reasons she never added the 'sweet dreams' connection that was so prevalent for couples who were apart...those types of dreams were not possible for him currently, but she always thought 'someday'.

Chapter 14
Wrong Number

As soon as Les hung up on Kevin her phone rang again. Presuming it was Kevin forgetting to share something else she answered with, "Do you miss me sweetheart?"

The other voice on the phone replied with, "That's a nice greeting and as a matter of fact I do." She could not recognize the voice and its ominous tone at first, but when it followed with, "How is your boyfriend?" It became unmistakable and she responded with an abrupt, "What do you want?"

Anson in mock shock recoiled with, "Hey, I liked the previous tone much better" and in an even creepier tone cooed, "I think we're about to become close friends."

The thought almost made her vomit and she now recoiled with another, "What do you want?"

Anson replied, "Just trying to sort out a few things about your boyfriend's past life or should I say lives. I'm sure there could be a number of people who would find it fascinating, but I know it would not be pleasant."

It was Les' turn to be the protective bear looking as though it was her own cub. While she wasn't a 'mama bear', anyone trying to harm Kevin would need to come through her first. She responded with as strong an accusation as she could muster, "If you do anything to harm Kevin...well, I'm not sure what I'd do."

Anson countered with, "Slow down, I just want to talk. I hear we're both in Dallas. I'm staying at the Fairmont in the Presidential Suite (wasn't that an aspirational gesture) why don't you come over around 7:30 PM." He noted some hesitancy in her accepting the invite and added. "The Secret Service detail is with me here, so you need not worry about your safety."

Les knew meeting with Anson was a bad idea, but so wanted to protect Kevin at all costs. She knew there were people out there who wanted to cause Miles harm, and if his new cover was blown, they would be lining up to take their shots.

She reluctantly accepted with, "I'll be there."

While she dreaded what might transpire over the course of the evening... it had to be done.

Chapter 15
Whose Side Are You on

Bryce hated to make this call but did not know what else he could do. Resigning from his post as Chief of Staff for one of the more successful politicians would raise many more questions about Anson's dealings, and while it would provide temporary relief for Bryce, he was sure his past involvement in prior schemes would lead to his being subpoenaed or worse arrested. He knew what he had to do.

Special Agent Withers answered his phone with a cheery, "Hello Bryce, what's up?"

Bryce said simply, "We need to talk."

Withers acknowledged this with an, "OK, can you get to a secure phone. I'm not sure what you're about to tell me, but I'm thinking it will need to be secure."

Bryce said he'd call Withers back in 15 minutes. Unbeknownst to either of them Leslie was on her way to see the Secretary in his hotel in Dallas. Things were beginning to happen quickly.

Chapter 16
The Man I Fell in Love With

Liz answered her phone hoping it was Kevin or Leslie, but it was neither. The voice on the other side of the phone said, "Is this Elizabeth Flaherty?"

Liz countered, "Yes, to whom and I speaking?" Her gut told her this was a typical solicitation call.

The other voice added, "I am Special Agent Walker and I'm with the FBI, and I'm working on a case involving your son. Kevin."

Her heart sank, she knew the more people who knew about his past the more danger he could be in, even in this case, the FBI. She said only, "Go on."

Walker added, "We have reason to believe your ex-fiancé is attempting to uncover information about your son that could be damaging to both your son and others, but to our nation as well. Do you have any idea why the Secretary would do such a thing?"

Liz muttered, "Because he's a vindictive son of a bitch! What can I do to help you investigation Special Agent?"

Walker in a tone that was all business began with, "I am certain there will be plenty to do once our case against the Secretary is filed and prosecution begins, but at this point there's only one thing you need to do. Get ahold of your son's girlfriend and stop her from following through with an invite he's extended to her to meet with him in his hotel at 7:30 PM tonight. We're concerned with what his intentions might be and don't want to 'show our hand just yet'."

Liz looked at her watch, it was 7:28 in Dallas, "I'll call right now." Both times she pleaded for Les to pick-up, and both times it rolled to voicemail. "Dammit!"

A concerned Jim Flaherty asked what was wrong and received a briefing from his wife. As looked at Jim he stood up and in a single motion grabbed his hat and moved towards the door with a look of absolute certainty. His renewed confidence was a joy, and a little bit of a turn on for Liz, who had witnessed her husband wither over the years of Kevin's exile from their lives. Now puzzled she asked, "Where you are going?"

Jim looked back with a look that was half determination and half pure anger, "To Dallas, I'm sorry, but that man needs his ass kicked, and I feel like doing it."

At that moment she was suddenly reminded of where Kevin had gotten his courage and empathy from, it was not just her as many had believed during her pain-staking search for her son, a search Jim had excused himself from early in the process. He just could not be reminded every day that his only child, his son was either dead or somewhere he needed help.

She got up and quickly grabbed her husband and added, "I know you would and its one of the things I love about you, but right now I think we have some other things to do from right here."

A calmer Jim looked at the woman he had always loved, so much that when they had been apart, he actually felt pain, "It is, you do?"

Liz nodded, "Yes, now more than ever."

A focused Jim countered with, "Should we call Kevin?"

Deep in thought Liz pondered, "Is there anything he could do other than worry? Besides, I'm quite sure Les can handle herself against that weasel."

Jim was dying to ask, what did you ever see in that guy? But thought better of it. There were certain questions you didn't want to know the answer to.

Chapter 17
Anything

As Leslie walked down the hallway towards the Suite, she thought of two things: 1) she could never let any harm to Kevin, and 2) where were the previously referenced Secret Service detail. Another thought was how she had witnessed Kevin able to navigate through many more difficult situations in their short time together and wanted to demonstrate she was up to the task as well.

She began her knock and the door opened immediately. He had either been anticipating her arrival or had been peering out the security peep hole. In a single gesture Anson ushered her in and offered her a drink.

Les replied, "No thank you. I cannot stay long."

A disappointed Anson reacted, "That's too bad. Ever since our initial introduction I've been looking forward to spending some quality time together."

The reference to quality time sickened Les and she added, "No, I have a friend waiting for me in the lobby." There was no friend in the lobby or anywhere else nearby and was an attempt to keep Anson a bit off-guard.

Anson suggested, "Perhaps you can't text them and let them know you expect the meeting may go longer than you anticipated." The suggestion felt more like a direct order.

Les persisted, "No, now what did you want to talk about, and by the way, where is the Secret Service detail you referenced over the phone?"

Anson in almost a joking tone responded, "Well, they wouldn't be very secret if you could see them all the time."

A more serious Les proceeded with, "Now what was it that you wanted to discuss with me?"

Anson gathered himself and began with, "What would you say if I told you someone wanted to bring forward the past lives of your boyfriend, and that this information could bring mortal harm to him or his family." Anson let the words settle in and began the slightest sense of arousal begin to hit.

Les digested the words and responded with, "I suppose I'd tell that person I'd do anything to not let that happen."

Anson seized on the word and repeated it, "Anything?' as his gaze fell onto the bedroom. The problem with people like him is they presume others feel the same way as he does, and for Anson it was never about the intimate beauty of making love to another, it was about the power he wielded over that other person.

The bedroom was staged with a hidden camera that would record their time together. he knew the anger it would create with Elizabeth to see her future daughter-in-law in bed with her ex-fiancé, and while the hurt was the primary goal, he even thought it could bring them back together.

He approached Les and put his hand on one of her hips, "Would you be willing to have sex with that person?" His other hand placed on the opposite hip served as leverage to pull her near to him. She in an almost seductive manner whispered "No."

This reaction surprised Anson and he pulled her even closer and pressed his lips against hers. Les had already determined she was more athletic than her adversary and was able to push him away. In an almost single move, that Kevin would have been proud of, she brought her knee into his groin, "I said no!" Then as Anson was doubled over in pain, she delivered an uppercut to his chin. He went down like a sack of potatoes.

The door to the adjoining room burst open and twp Secret Service agents rushed in with guns drawn and placed handcuff on Les with her hands behind her back. One of them declared, "You're under arrest."

A relatively calm, Les asked, "What am I being charged with?" The Secret Service agent replied, "For assaulting a federally elected or appointed leader."

Just then there was a knock at the door leading to the hallway. The other Secret Service agent opened the door and Special agent Walker strode in. He flashed his credentials and introduced his two associates. Les recognized him from her meeting with Rosie and suddenly felt as though the good guys were here and nodded towards Les in manner confirming her assessment.

We're investigating federal charges against a cabinet member who is using their influence in an illegal manner, and we'd like a private word with the witness before she is taken into custody.

The word 'custody' spoken by Walker confirmed to Les she would be taken into custody, and she flashed a small smile knowing it was all worth it.

A still shaky Anson was able to finally at least sit up and declared, "This woman assaulted me in my own room."

A calm yet, determined Walker offered, "Mr. Secretary we're interviewing members of your staff, subpoenas are being issued on personal information you may have on past indiscretions, and you former Chief of Staff has turned as witness on our behalf. Anything else you might say at this point can be used in our investigation.

A disheartened Anson asked, "Am I being charged?"

Walker responded, "No sir, not at this time, but I do have a summons here from the President to be in his office at 8 AM tomorrow morning."

As Walker and Les stepped into the adjoining room she handed him the recording device she had on during her conversation with Anson. She asked if it would be enough to put him away for an extended period. He responded with, "Perhaps, but I'm sure the President will deal with him more harshly than a court of law could." He paused, "And by the way, the President would like to meet with you, Kevin and his parents at your convenience. Unfortunately, it cannot be in the Oval Office, but we'll arrange a more discrete location."

Les smiled and said, "I'm not sure my guy will go for it. He doesn't care much for attention."

Walker smiled back and said "I'm sure you can be convincing, and oh, by the way, can I have your phone? I need to let him know if he calls that you're in custody."

Chapter 18
Consequences

It was now close to 11 PM in Florida when Elizabeth's phone finally rang. Neither she nor Jim had even considered falling asleep, they were worried sick about the meeting Les was attending with Anson. Liz felt a bond with Les that could never be broken, she considered her one of the reasons her son had returned to her and would be forever grateful.

She saw Les's number on her screen and jumped on the call-in seconds flat. She gushed, "We've been worried sick waiting to hear from you." The pause in response, though only momentary, was enough to create anxiety with Liz. She repeated, "Les?" Now Jim moved in towards with a concerned expression as well, he still wanted a piece of Anson.

Finally, a male voice came on the call, "Ms. Flaherty?"

Liz could not contain herself, and Jim hearing only fragments of the conversation was now on his feet. Liz responded, "Where is she...what have you done with her?"

The male voice in a calming manner said. "Ms. Flaherty, this is Special Agent Walker of the FBI. Les is fine and is in custody as we speak."

Lix had a million questions in her mind, but could only muster, "Custody, why?"

Walker with pride clearly in his voice, "For assaulting a federal cabinet member." He let that sink in and Liz repeated it to Jim who shouted, "That's my girl."

Walker continued saying he wanted to tell them the rest of the story but wanted to know how he could contact Kevin. His mother knew he was on a flight to San Diego, and they arranged to have an agent meet him as he exited the plane.

Walker went on with the complete story. How they were tracking Anson's actions, and knew he was looking to undermine their son's future by exposing his past. Of course, there would be a multitude of charges available for consideration, but that had been his primary concern.

Liz asked if Anson would go to jail, and Walker explained he was meeting with the President at 8 AM tomorrow morning and would likely be stripped of his position. He expected there might be some form of plea bargaining arranged with Secretary Gamble, but he would be out of their collective lives.

"He better," boasted Jim. "Or we'll sick Les on him again." They all shared a laugh and Liz and Jim expressed their gratitude to Walker and his team.

As they were hanging up Walker remembered one last thing, "Oh, by the way, the President has asked for a meeting with the four of you. Said there was some unfinished business. Unfortunately, due to your son's background it needs to be done away from the Oval Office, but someone from the white House will be in contact."

The call ended and Jim and Liz looked at one another with parental pride. Jim spoke first with, "How did we raise such a good man?"

Liz replied, "Simple, he had a good role model." There was not a better compliment she could have given her husband, and then in a sterner voice added, "He better put a ring on that girl's finger."

Chapter 19
San Diego

As soon as Kevin's Delta flight touched down and taxied toward its gate, he had a premonition something was not right. There was no voicemail from Les saying how much she missed him, and she was all he could think of during the flight. It was very early, and Kevin tried to dismiss it as time differences, etc.

As the plane reached the gate the intercom came on and said will all passengers remain seated. Will Mr. Flaherty please exit the plane now. This was never a good sign. They rarely asked you off the plane in this manner with good news.

As Kevin got to the passenger boarding and exiting bridge/ramp he unconsciously began to jog. Whatever the news is he needed to hear it fast. As he entered the concourse, he saw two men in suits who were clearly law enforcement, he presumed FBI waiting for him. Before they presented their credentials and introduced themselves in a near panic said, "Is she OK?"

One of the Agents grabbed him by the arm and attempted to usher him along with them, "Please just come with us Mr. Flaherty."

Kevin was not about to be led anywhere until the question was answered. He now pleaded, "I'll go anywhere you want, just tell me she's OK?"

The agents were immediately sympathetic to his concern. The senior agent nodded to his associate in a way that said tell him. The other agent spoke clearly, "Your mother and girlfriend are both fine. Your girlfriend is in federal custody."

Kevin sighed a tremendous sigh of relief and then with a perplexed look muttered, "Custody?"

The two agents ushered him into a private meeting room adjacent to the Delta VIP Club.

Chapter 20
The Comeuppance

As Anson was ushered into the Oval Office, the very office he had dreamed of occupying, he was overwhelmed by not only the gravity of the situation, but in how badly the odds were stacked against him. of course, as with most culprits or victims with his psychological profile, it was never his fault...and in this case his tortured soul had plenty of people to draw from.

The door opened to what appeared to be a meeting that was already taking place. In the room was the President, his Chief of Staff, the Vice President, the Attorney General, and the two individuals he had completely not expected to see, Special Agent Withers and Anson's Chief of Staff, Bryce. The Attorney General being provided a briefing the day before from the two of them had suggested they be "in the room." It might keep Anson from 'fabricating' facts, as he had been known to do.

Anson was still smarting from the physical beating he had received from Les's right fist and more importantly her right knee. The swelling in his groin had gone down after a night with multiple ice packs, but the sting of being "taken down" by a woman who was 70 lbs lighter than him remained.

The President looked angry, and indeed he was. His anger, while primarily focused on Anson, and the damage his behavior could cause his Administration, but with the leaders of his party and significant donors to his campaign that had mandated he throw Anson a bone when his Cabinet was being formed. The 2nd tier cabinet position seemed harmless enough. It had a good echelon of smart, committed public servants supporting Secretary Gamble that would make sure the real work got done.

The President had recently admonished his own Chief of Staff for missing two major red flags on the job Anson was or was not doing. His two most senidirectors in HHS have recently resigned, and if proper exit interviews would have been conducted, they would have known how out of control the Secretary had become. Nevertheless, they now had a much bigger mess to clean-up, and the President swore to himself that he would never allow himself forced into being ever used in the same manner again, and he would take action later in the day to assure it would never happen.

The President did not rise from his desk to shake Anson's hand, he simply gestured to a chair for him to sit in and began with an abrupt, "I trust you know everyone in the room?" Anson smiled and nodded at each of the occupants, except for Bryce and Special Agent Withers. While he had hoped there might be some friends in the room, not one of them smiled back.

The President restarted his remarks with, "I think we all know what we're here for..."

In an unbelievable interruption to the President Anson proclaimed, "And I look forward to some constructive feedback so that we can get back to the important work of running our great country." He still thought he could talk himself out of trouble.

The President shook his head vigorously in the negative, "No, that is not what this is about at all. You've demonstrated, quite clearly you are not up to the task at hand with the HHS. In fact, there is not a position within this administration you're qualified, or should I say, unqualified to perform." After Anson's initial interruption the President wanted to add delusional to his remarks but thought better of it without a trained psychologist in the room. Instead, he paused... "You've become an embarrassment."

Again, Anson took the opportunity to inject with, "I look forward to the dialog."

This time the President shook his a little less vigorously and added, "I doubt it...and from this point forward I ask, no demand that you only respond to direct questions."

Anson nodded and finally held his tongue.

The President nodded and made a brief statement that ended with, "Of the numerous transgressions you've committed as Secretary, and as we're learning more about in your time in the Senate, the one that intrigues me the most is you effort to unveil the past of one Kevin Flaherty, can you enlighten us on why you felt the need to pursue this random course of action?"

Anson responded flatly to somehow legitimize his actions, "National security."

Everyone in the room maintained their poker faces, except the Vice President, she had served with Gamble in the Senate and was familiar with these types of outlandish comments, who covered her mouth to suppress a laugh. The President shot her a scolding look, while he understood the unintended humor of the comment, but needed the meeting needed to remain serious.

The President followed with, "You do understand that while you've taken an oath to protect the Constitution et al, it is not your role to investigate these matters, and this Administration sees the target of your alleged investigation to be the complete opposite of a threat to our country and has in fact served courageously in a number of roles." He paused briefly and held up his hand signaling it was not Anson's time to speak, "And furthermore, one of our witnesses, your former Chief of Staff, shared with us that he informed you of this very issue previously."

Anson attempted to respond, but the President put up the stop sign once again.

The President went on, "I have neither the time or interest to review your complete list of transgressions. I have directed the Attorney to prosecute the case against you as strongly as is possible, and with the full support of this office. As of this moment you are no longer part of this Administration, and plan to have a Press Conference at 4 PM this afternoon to address the topic with the American people. This leaves you 7 hours to decide what I will tell them. This meeting is over."

The Attorney general walked over to a crestfallen Anson Gamble and said simply, "Please join me in my office."

Chapter 21
Reunion

Kevin had been fully briefed by the two Agents on everything that had transpired. His initial action had been wanting if to not kill Gamble but do inflict major harm. While this was an almost typical male reaction to another male threatening a loved one, Kevin's training and discipline likely would have kicked in before he fully executed.

His emotions that he directed towards Les were much different...

Kevin started again with, "What were you thinking?"

Les gushed, "Well clearly I wasn't. He suggested some harm being done to you and your family and I just snapped. "I'm sorry, were you worried?"

Kevin in a more measured tone, "My antenna went up when I didn't have a few texts from you last night. And then when the flight crew announced everyone should remain seated except for me. And then the two FBI agents waiting inside the terminal was another nice touch."

Les replied in order: "Oh, oh, oh no, I'm sorry. That was all Walker's doing."

Kevin solemnly, "He's a good man, one of the best...in all, it was one of the scariest moments of my life."

This from a man who had been in some pretty scary moments. "Les, I'm not sure what I'd do if anything..."

Les agreed, "I know, I know...neither of us needs that scenario now."

Kevin with an exclamation point, "But I'm really proud of how you kicked his ass!"

Chapter 22
Sprinting to the Finish Line

Towards the end of the call Les asked how his first two meetings had gone. She knew the first two were the "easy" ones. Not to diminish their importance to Kevin, but the profiles were simpler with positive outcomes expected.

The next two were key in allowing Kevin to live his life 'guilt free', if there is such a thing, and with some of his personal demons put to rest. He had often thought of the line from Doc Holiday in the film Tombstone, "There is no normal life, there's just life."

As he left the private conference room, he was met again by the two FBI agents, "Don't you guys have anything better to do?" Kevin quipped.

This time Special Agent Cole had an equal response, "No sir...Walker suggested we give you a lift."

Kevin looked the two men over and asked, "Either of you men in the Corps?"

In unison they announced, "Semper Fi!"

Kevin nodded, "I thought so...let's go!"

Chapter 23
No Escape

As Anson and the Attorney General made their way to his office, the Justice Department is .72 or roughly ¾ miles from the White House, he noticed a change in the entourage that usually accompanied them. Usually there was a security detail of Secret Service and Capitol Police followed by a few of their support staff, but this time it was different.

Anson's Secret Service detail, while always smaller and deferring to the Attorney General was now gone, it had already been cancelled, there were none of his staff, even Bryce was no longer present, and there were two additions, Federal Marshall's. Even though formal charges had not been brought, he was considered the culprit in many crimes and misdemeanors and was considered a high flight risk.

As they exited the Black Suburban and began the ascent up the 44 steps that led to the building in which the Supreme Court is housed with the words adorning the entrance, "Equal Justice to All," Anson caught the AG's eye and in nodding towards the Federal Marshal's asked, "Is this really necessary?" The Attorney General's curt response was, "Yes, the President insisted on it!

Anson realized now that he was part of a choreographed "perp" or perpetrator walk. As always there was news media on hand with the question why two Federal Marshall's are escorting the Attorney General and HHS Secretary. It created a buzz that would only be quieted by the President's Press Conference later that day.

Once they entered the building the entire entourage was ushered into a mid-size conference room adjacent to the Attorney General's office. There they were joined by two additional attorneys from the Justice Department. As always, an impatient Anson offered: "Isn't there a way we can work this out?"

The Attorney General looked over at Anson and in an extremely measured tone responded, "Well, yes there is and here are the President's terms:

1. You will resign immediately with a statement we prepare on your behalf.

2. You will accept a guilty plea for every crime charged against you.

3. All funds in your past campaign accounts will be used as reparations to injured parties of your actions.

4. You will be forbidden to ever hold public office ever again.

The Attorney General paused and allowed the words to sink in. A thoroughly defeated man sat across from him, and while it was hard to scrape the arrogance from a man like Anson Gamble, it had been done in convincing style during what amounted to less than 5 minutes. His world was crumbling and at this point all he good do was beg for leniency. He looked over to the AG and asked, "Will this mean jail time?"

Again, a measured response from the Attorney General, "That is not for me to presume. A judge will be assigned to carry out you're sentencing. However, I would say a guilty plea will lessen the maximum sentencing that is permitted for similar crimes."

Anson was near tears now, "Can you speculated what the maximum would entail?"

The Attorney General said simply, "I've witnessed similar crimes that were sentenced for 20 years."

Anson followed with, "And a plea-bargained case?"

The Attorney General, "If I were to speculate 5 years with no time off for 'good behavior', and remember you have until 4 PM to accept this offer. Otherwise, we will begin prosecuting to the full extent of the law, beginning with a complete freeze of your assets."

Anson closed his eyes and shook his head, "I accept the conditions!"

Word spread quickly through the core team involved in this investigation. Special Agent Walker had a brief conference call with Les, still in Dallas and Jim and Liz in Florida on the outcome of the hearing and then called Kevin directly in California. While they were all positive with the news, none were gleeful, Walker understood and appreciated their perspective. It was in reality, a sad day for our country.

When Liz and Jim hung up their phone she turned and said, "I love you and thank you."

Jim responded quickly with, "I do too and for what?"

Liz continued, "For never asking what I saw in that man."

Jim took a long time before responding, "Liz, we were both broken in losing Kevin. To be honest I took some solace in unexpected sources myself. All that matters is we're back together."

Liz feeling much better... "What does taking solace mean?"

Chapter 24
Work to Be Done

Kevin asked his newfound escorts to park a block away from his destination in La Jolla, California. La Jolla is an upscale beach community in Southern California that while retaining some of its "beachy" elements was for the most part a version of 'Beverly Hills' on the water...most Americans would find much of it "jaw dropping" in the picturesque vistas and high-end shops.

He met his appointment at the Brick and Bell, a favorite among the locals and tourists alike. He understood why Pamela Ruiz- Van Landingham would want to meet at a neutral spot. Her first husband, the pilot Kevin had tried to rescue was James (Jim) "Vamos" Ruiz. They had only been married less than a year when his F-4 Phantom was shot down and had no children, which made Kevin's work somewhat easier.

Lieutenant Ruiz was another product of the Naval Academy. As his call name would suggest, he was in a proverbial rush to get wherever he was going. He had big plans for his immediate family, as well as the overall Latino community. Kevin had always admired the commitment to family within their community.

Pamela after urging Kevin to call her Pam urged Kevin to sit down in the corner of the coffee shop that was away from the prying eyes in her new community. She admitted to loving Jim very much and seemed somehow embarrassed by her new life. The mourning period for Pam had been relatively short, and she had remarried another Marine pilot who had been a close friend of Jim's. It had been suggested by some that Pam may have had a relationship with the friend prior to Jim's demise.

It was Kevin's turn to tell his side of Jim's last minutes on this earth. He had ejected and landed in a heavily wooded, near jungle area in the north. When the call came into the Marine Recovery Unit Kevin knew his team was in a race to get to the pilot first. It was a race against time for Kevin's team and the pilot, with the loser getting an all-expense paid vacation at the infamous Hanoi Hilton. A spot no pilot was in a rush to visit.

As the two-helicopter team approached the downed pilot he was advised to deploy green smoke to direct them to their exact location. Kevin typically instructed his copter to perform a flyover, it was his way of getting the lay of the land. The other copter was to fly wide circles around the extraction site, with the hope of seeing the approaching NVA, and if necessary, delaying their approach. Once Kevin had determined the proper course of action Kevin was patched into the pilot.

Kevin spoke first, "Vamos', this is Halo 1. We're coming to get you." He was allowed to use their call sign, but Kevin's name was not permitted...there was a bounty on him.

Vamos - "You're a sight for sore eyes."

Halo 1 - "We need to move quickly, are you capable of moving in a rapid pace?"

Vamos - "Roger that."

Halo 1 - "There's a small clearing about 25 meters NE of your location. Do you read? Copy?"

Vamos - "Roger that...on my way."

There had been no names exchanged, bit Jim was sure it was the famous Kevin Flaherty who had come to get him and it was most reassuring.

Halo 1 - When you've reached the edge of the clearing deploy red smoke. It will be our signal to begin the extraction. We have not seen any 'bads' in the vicinity but would prefer getting in/out as quickly as possible. Be prepared to jump in as soon as we make contact."

Vamos - "Roger that."

As the copter began its run it all felt good, just the way they'd planned it. He saw a lone figure emerge from the cover of the thick vegetation and move towards their intended landing site. It wasn't really a "landing site." In these situations, the copter never fully touched down. A skillful pilot, in the case Donald 'Daffy' Drake or 'Daf' for short, was one of the best, would hover a yard or so above the ground. It gave the copter a jump in leaving the scene as quickly as possible.

Everything had gone according to plan...and then Kevin heard the 'crack' of a high-powered rifle. The moment it hit Vamos in the back he knew they were in trouble. Kevin announced to the entire team...active sniper! The door gunner scanned the vegetation and saw another puff of smoke. This time the shot glanced harmlessly off a part of the copter. "Sniper identified!" He unloaded 50 rounds in the general area where the smoke had appeared, and satisfied with his response, "Sniper neutralized."

As Kevin pulled Vamos in he instructed Daf to exit the field and return to base ASAP. During this brief flight Vamos thanked Kevin for coming to get him, talked about his beautiful wife and said he was proud to be a Marine. He died in route.

Pam listened intently and remained silent for a minute or so, without shedding a tear, her mourning process had come and gone she stated plainly, "He was a good man." Kevin nodded. She went on to ask, "Why do you continue to beat yourself up over this...? It seems like you did everything you could do."

Kevin pondered the question before answering, "I'm not sure. I guess if I'd done everything, I could do Jim would be sitting here having a cup of coffee with us." He paused, "I don't like losing, especially when it costs another man his life."

Pam studied him, "I didn't think men like you existed, well maybe in the movies, and it's reassuring to know you're out there. As far as I'm concerned your conscience should be clear."

All Kevin could say was, "Thank you."

Chapter 25
Sorting Things Out

Les was back in the small conference room at the Federal facility. Once again, the door opened and in walked Special Agent Walker. Les was no longer shackled, and as Walker moved towards her, he held out his hand, "Thank you, all charges against you have now been dropped and you are free to go." Walker allowed himself a wry smile, "In fact, based upon the sentencing of the Secretary, you might be eligible to file a claim against him."

Les returned the smile more widely and responded with, "Oh, I think I've had enough dealings with him, and besides, I imagine the list may be quite long without the shenanigans he attempted to pull with me. Thank you for everything though."

This time it was Walker's turn to respond in a more genuine manner, "I suppose you're right...but it's me who should be thanking you. If we hadn't caught him now there's no telling how much more damage he could have to the current administration and the country."

Les nodded and said simply, "You're welcome."

Walker rubbed his hands together, "Where to now?"

Les announced, "Back to Gainesville to Kevin's parents. I hope to see Kevin late tonight or early in the morning. He has one more meeting in California." Les paused and contemplated the next question. "Can I ask one more question of you? Walker nodded. "You knew my husband. I miss him, but feel extremely lucky to have Kevin in my life...do you know what I mean?"

A more serious Walker recalling Sam Grant, "Yes, he was one of the best. He walked the walk and talked the talk. It was not only important for Sam to catch the bad guys, but he also needed to set an example that there were good guys in the fight. Unfortunately, it made him and ultimately you a target." Les listened intently, she knew he was not finished, "As far as you are being 'lucky', bullshit!"

Les straightened up in her chair, "You might be 'fortunate', but you and Kevin deserve all the happiness you can find...and then some, and you know what, I am 100% sure Sam would agree."

Les simply said, "Thank you!"

Walker looked down at his shoes, "Few people know what I'm about to tell you, but my father was an FBI agent who was killed in the line of duty. My mother and I mourned his loss deeply. She remarried quickly, a little too quickly for some, she wanted me to have a strong man in my life. He will never replace my father, but my dad made a huge difference in my life...he was an FBI agent as well."

Les wrapped it up with, "Thank you for sharing, I hope we meet again."

Walker, "I do to."

Chapter 26
Do the Right Thing

As Kevin and the two agents drove towards Oceanside, California, which is near the Camp Pendleton Marine Base, they were reminded the Presidential Press Conference was coming on and located a news channel to listen:

My fellow American's, I come to you today to ask for your collective forgiveness and to solemnly pledge to never let what I am about to share with you happen again...not on my watch.

I accepted the resignation of my Secretary of Health & Human Services today, Mr. Anson Gamble. I wish I could say Mr. Gamble was a good public servant, but the truth is just the opposite. He used his current and prior positions in government for not only personal gain, but to inflict pain upon his fellow citizens. The extent of these dealings I was made fully aware of by my members of the Department of Justice, they were supported in their actions by private citizens, who while remaining unnamed represent the best our country has to offer.

Now to the important part of my comments...you may ask who could allow someone this despicable into a position as lofty as this cabinet position. Well, I am ashamed to say you're looking at him. In becoming your President, I needed the help of others in significant ways. In order to secure this level of support we make promises, and as a result the vetting process can be ignored if carried out at all. My administration did just that and I promise it will never happen again.

But that's not enough, the next time you step into the ballot box or whatever voting choice you elect to use, I ask that you remember what I did here. In fact the day before our next Presidential Election I will actively remind you of it. My only hope is I can demonstrate that beyond this horrible act of negligence I did enough good to earn or retain your vote.

God bless you and these United States of America!

As the President left the podium the four private citizens...Jim, Liz. Les and Kevin took a moment to feel good about themselves and the country they loved.

For Kevin, the car had stopped for his final meeting of the day.

Chapter 27
Mission Accomplished

It had all led to this...his personal struggles, a second chance at life and love and now the completion of a vow he had made to a man he had hardly known that mattered to him most. As he walked the last few yards to a modest home barely outside the gates to the largest marine base in the United States, he felt a sense of foreboding and exhilaration.

Camp Pendleton was originally purchased for $4,239,000 in 1942 and included 122,798 acres, if it were private property today, wedged between Orange and San Diego counties, it is estimated to be worth $1.7 billion, a multiple of over 400 times. Each day the population on the camp expands to over 70,000 military and civilian personnel.

Michelle Foster never wanted to leave Oceanside, it held too many good memories, but it had created some challenges in raising her son, Deacon. Deacon's father, Derek "Deacon" Foster was a Naval Academy graduate who served his country admirably and in living up to the expectations of his own father, Rear Admiral Nathan Foster (ret). She was somehow looking forward to meeting Kevin but wasn't sure why.

She answered the door to a stranger who seemed familiar at the same time. Kevin greeted her simply with, "Michelle, I'm Kevin Flaherty." It was odd, but he was not completely used to his original name. He had gone so long without it that it still seemed a bit foreign to him.

Michelle quickly welcomed him, "Please come in, I've been looking forward to meeting you." The comment was partially true. She really wasn't sure how to feel.

As Kevin sat down on the modest couch and looked around, he asked, "Will Deacon be joining us?"

Michelle grimaced, "I'm afraid Deacon does not hold the memory of his father in a very good place. He feels as though his father abandoned us in the service of his country."

Kevin nodded his head and confided something he had never done before to a stranger, "I'm sorry, I guess my parents felt the same way." She looked at him with a puzzled expression. He went on, "The next rescue after Deac's I was badly wounded, and the chopper left me behind. I was reported KIA but was taken to a POW camp. I was reunited with my parents only last year."

Michelle still looked puzzled, "Why the long gap between..."

Kevin shook his head, "It's a long story, and frankly, most of it I'm not at liberty to tell, I'm sorry."

Michelle now in a more concerned tone, "They are thrilled now, but they went through hell."

Just then the sound of a back door opening and closing entered the room they were in. Both he and Michelle looked up expectantly, and what Kevin saw caused him to shudder. Other than the long hair it could have been the father he had met under dire circumstances so many years ago.

Michelle was the first to speak, "Deacon, this is the man I was telling you about..." Deacon acted as though he could have cared less and merely shrugged his shoulders.

Kevin added, "I've been looking forward to meeting you, and....the resemblance to you dad is staggering." Deacon quietly nodded but made no further movement towards or away from the two of them. Kevin persisted, "I have some things I'd like to share with you and your mother."

Deacon in a stern voice, "Listen mister whatever your name is, I don't know if you're here to take a walk down memory lane or assuage your guilt, but my mom and I don't need it. We've been through this act dozens of times and no matter what your intentions I end up feeling like shit, so which one is it today?" A shocked Michelle could only look on, as harsh as the words sounded, they were accurate.

Kevin took a long look at the young man and replied simply, "Neither." He waited a few more seconds before adding, "I'm here because I promised your father I would and to deliver this..." Kevin reached into his jacket pocket and pulled out what appeared to be an envelope. It was badly soiled.

Deacon still scowling, "What's that?"

Kevin taking a few steps forward, but not invading his personal space replied, "It's a letter from your dad. He asked me with his last breath to deliver it and I promised him I would." He took a few steps closer and handed it to him, "It belongs to you, and my mission is complete."

As Kevin stepped towards the door a suddenly surprised voice said, "What am I supposed to do with this?"

Kevin turned back again, "Well, if it were me, I'd read it."

Deacon persisted, "And what are all these stains."

Kevin tried to think of a delicate was to phrase it but couldn't, "His blood...he was pretty banged up."

Deacon slowly sat down and stared at the letter. He had never felt this close to the man.

Chapter 28
Lessons Learned

The letter read as follows...

My Deacon,

If you are reading this letter, I have broken my promise to you and your mother, a promise to return and be part of your life. I am truly sorry and know there is nothing I can say in this letter to make up for it. I will try my best to share a few things that meant much to me in my upbringing, and i hope they will help you now.

First and foremost, your mother is not to blame. She wanted none of this, and in fact had tried to talk me out of my desire to be a combat pilot. At this point i must agree with her, another lesson learned. I should have listened to her about a lot of things...she's smart and will care about you more than anyone. You must be smarter than I was on this point.

Secondly, someone once told me a long time ago 'if you don't know where you are going, any road will get you there'. I pray you will figure this out on your own and do not feel compelled to follow my dreams, create your own. Mom will help you along the way, but it must be your dream. I know you will succeed in your chosen path.

A life is a gift that can be shared with many others. I was fortunate to have a multitude of friends and family who loved and cared about me. There were times I took these gifts for granted, assumed they would always be there, do not make that mistake, and remember there will always be certain people you can count on regardless of the situation. I had planned on being one of them, it is now even more important for you to find others who will embrace that role.

Finally, I will choose someone to deliver this letter who I think can help fill in some of the gaps I've left behind. They will not be a father figure, maybe not even a man, but someone who I believe shows true character in the face of adversity, a strong sense of right and wrong, good versus evil, and most importantly the ability to love another person in a powerful, long-lasting manner.

I wish I could be there to see it all unfold, and maybe I'll see it from afar, but I wish you the best in everything you choose. it's out there waiting for you...now go get it.

Your Dad

Chapter 29
Chosen

After handing the letter to Deacon Kevin lingered, in all honesty he did not know what the right thing to do was...on the one hand he felt almost as though he was trespassing on an intimate moment for Deacon and his mother, but something in his inner core told him to stay.

Deacon continued to stare at the letter as if he needed to read it multiple times in order to comprehend it. His mother moved slowly next to him and put her hand on his shoulder, and while she desperately wanted to read the letter, she knew it belonged to Deacon.

Finally, after what seemed an eternity Deacon looked up squarely into the eyes of the man who had delivered the letter and asked, "What do you think?"

Kevin choosing his words carefully, "You'll have to be more specific?"

Deacon explained, "Your role?"

Kevin in a deliberate fashion, "I thought my role was to deliver it. I apologize for the time it has taken and tried to explain the reasons to your mother. Beyond that I have no role that I am aware of...and no, I have not read the letter."

Deacon stood slowly and moved towards Kevin, he held the letter out towards Kevin and said in a halting tone, "Can you read the second to last paragraph?"

Kevin accepted the letter and was temporarily overcome with the gravity of the assignment, and questioned how his father had been able to pass on this role to someone he had just met...perhaps out of desperation? Was he up to the task?

As his mind flickered about in a whirlwind of thoughts it finally came to him, why it had taken so long to deliver... "and most importantly the ability to love another person in a powerful, long-lasting manner." Until just recently Kevin could not have been that person, it had only been the insertion of Les into his life that would complete the needed list of requirements.

Kevin absorbed every word and handed it back to Deacon. He passed the letter to his mother, and she read it fighting back the tears. Many would call it 'divine intervention'. Kevin was not sure. He simply nodded at the young man who was now at a 'crossroads'. As so beautifully put in the Bob Seger song, Roll Me Away.... 'I could go East, I could go West, it was all up to me to decide'.

Deacon met his nod with one of his own, sometimes the unspoken word can mean more that what is said, and these two nods meant they had both accepted their assignments. Deacon followed up with, "Please sit down." And in direct reference to his letter asked, "Would you mind telling me what road brought you here?" Kevin not knowing where to begin, simply started.

Losing all track of time, they were all startled by the knock at the door. Michelle opened it to find one of the FBI agents, "Excuse me mam." And then addressing Kevin, "Sir, if we do not leave immediately, you'll miss your flight 'home'." The word 'home' had a nice ring to it.

Kevin now turned back to Deacon and handed him a card, "This has every way to get a hold of me. I will be back to see you soon and have a few people I'd like you to meet." Next, in looking at Michelle, "If that's alright?" She quickly nodded; she had not felt this good in a long time.

As they stepped onto the front of the house the agent told Kevin, "We arranged for alternate transportation. Otherwise, you'd miss you flight. We're securing a landing zone 100 meters from here." This could only mean one thing, a helicopter. Kevin's last two rides had not been pleasant, the ride that left him for dead, and the extraction from the POW camp (and thankfully he had been unconscious for it). Nevertheless, he had managed to avoid them until just now.

The agent lifted a flare gun and fired green smoke to attract the inbound copter, the other agent fired a similar shot with red smoke to mark the temporary LZ. The symbolism was not lost on him. Only this time he was being rescued.

Deacon watched Kevin get in the car to go to meet the arriving helicopter. Who was this man? What did his father's letter mean to him? He turned to his mother, and they embraced one another. As Deacon began to quietly sob, he began to see a path for his life.

Kevin boarded the copter with some trepidation. The co-pilot recognizing it asked, "Don't like to fly?" Once again Kevin simply nodded. Once airborne, the co-pilot passed him a headset, "Someone wants to talk to you." He said hello and was relieved to hear Les say, "How did it go?" Kevin pondered the question and replied, "I think we have a son."

The words sent a warm feeling throughout her body. She had already begun thinking to herself that a child was the only thing missing in their lives, and while a biological birth at her and Kevin's ages seemed unlikely, the thought of adoption had entered her mind, "I can't wait to meet him."

Kevin smiling, "I'm sure he feels the same way. I'll tell you more when I get home." There's that word again, he was beginning to really like the sound of it.

Les excitedly, "Before I forget. We have a date with the President the day after tomorrow at Camp David."

Kevin just prior to handing back the headset responded with, "I'll check my calendar."

Chapter 30
Mission Accomplished

Kevin had promised Leslie a quiet night out the evening he returned and the night before they were to leave for Camp David. He asked if they could leave 30 minutes early on the way to the restaurant.

As Kevin pulled into their high school parking lot Leslie said, "This brings back a lot of memories?" Kevin gave her a smile and nodded his head as he took her hand. They strolled to the 50-yard line and took in the view. Kevin took hold of her other hand a kissed her gently on the cheek, "I'm going to do something I should have done a long time ago." Les looked a bit puzzled.

Suddenly he dropped to one knee and said, "Les, if you will agree to marry me it will make me the happiest man in the world, and..." Les was so excited and anxious to say yes that it was his turn to press his index finger against her lips. He went on, "And I promise to love and protect you the rest of our days."

After a pause and realizing it was her turn to respond she merely said, "You already have and YES!" She tugged him back up and planted a firm kiss on his face with the ear-to-ear grin. She exclaimed, "Finally!"

Kevin slipped the ring on her finger and shot back a sarcastic, "Well, we've been kind of busy."

Les observed the beautiful engagement ring and shouted, "I love it! When did you have time to shop?"

Kevin responded, "It's temporary, and no I didn't. It's my mom's original engagement ring. My Dad stepped up with a new one...maybe we're paying him too much."

Chapter 31
Camp David

C amp David is the country retreat for Presidents and their guests in Maryland. It was originally built in 1935 by the WPA and christened as Shangri-La by Franklin Roosevelt. It is 62 miles from the White House. In 1953 it was renamed Camp David by Dwight Eisenhower in honor of his father and grandson.

Kevin and the rest of the gang were picked up by a government issue black Suburban and escorted by two Federal Marshall vehicles. Kevin thought to himself, so much for a discreet departure/arrival. In route to the Gilmer Airport, a former federal air station, it now operated as a privately held airport and was perfect for this mission noted Kevin.

As they prepared to board the government issue Gulfstream V Kevin's phone rang. The voice on the other end asked, "Mr. Flaherty?"

Kevin responded with, "Mr. Flaherty is my father, I'm just Kevin."

The voice at the end of the line stammered, "OK, Kevin, this is Deacon."

Kevin stepped away from the rest of the group, "Deacon, great to hear from you."

Deacon wanted to ask Kevin for a favor and decided the direct approach seemed most sustainable. "After our conversation here other day I made some decisions about the path I want to follow."

Kevin almost shouted, "Terrific!! Where will it take you."

Deacon responded, "I want to go to the Naval Academy, like my dad and his dad. What do you think?"

Kevin said sharply, "I think it's a great idea,"

Deacon in asking for a favor, "I need some references. Can you help me with me with that?"

Kevin smirking, "I think I know someone who can help."

An elated Deacon, "Great! Hey, my mom needs to talk to you."

They boarded the plane and arrived at Camp David by mid-day. Meeting a President, especially one with a background like President Bayle, was an honor for anyone. His recent "confession" on national TV was driving positive feedback from not only his constituents...the American people but was serving as a lesson for politicians/leaders everywhere. He was quick to thank his guests for helping him look in the mirror.

At the end of the lunch, which was incredibly uncomfortable with accolades for Kevin, but it had his parents bursting with pride, the President asked if there was anything he could do for them. Kevin had two requests:

1) Could the FBI start a memorial fund in the names of his friend Sam Grant. Les had not known of his intentions and responded as only the widow of one and fiancé of the other might.

The President responded, "It shall be done, I will call the Attorney General as soon as you leave. What else?"

Kevin with as broad a smile as anyone had ever seen announced, "My godson would like to attend the Naval Academy."

He had not shared Michelle's request with anyone else.

Part 3 - The 30th Man

Chapter 1
Time Flies

A s Kevin reflected on the past four years, he was amazed on how many blessings had befallen on him and members of his immediate family:

- He and Les were more in love than ever,
- His parents were in the same position,
- The foundation was running beyond their hopes and dreams, with steadily growing contributions, and
- His past lives had stayed where they belong...in the past.

Moreover, in what he called, "an embarrassment of riches," his Godson was graduating from the Naval Academy.

The Naval Academy is known for graduating some of the best and brightest young people in the country. Graduates receive in four years a Bachelor of Science degree and are commission as Ensigns in the Navy or Second Lieutenant in the Marine Corps. Some of the more notable graduates include John McCain, Jimmy Carter, Alan Shepherd, David Robinson, and Chester Nimitz.

Deacon had chosen to be a Marine, not in any way against his father's choice of service, but to forge his own path. Plus, his GodFather was a Marine. For graduation, the Marines wore their black jackets and blue trousers for the ceremony. Les smiled remembering her comment to Kevin, then Jake, upon entering the US Embassy in Madrid. She still loved the look.

Michelle, Deacon's Mom, had made sure Kevin and Les were included as VIPs to the graduation ceremonies that included a formal ball the night before. She knew both had been surrogate parents in the best conceivable way. Les always remembered Deacon had a mother, and her role felt like a fusion of an aunt or older sister. Helping him figure out girls and some of his own emotions

It had been a wonderful day for all parties. Deacon had graduated high enough in his class to be able to choose his initial assignment. He had graduated with a BS in Software Engineering and had requested an assignment in the Pentagon. It had been granted and Michelle and Les were going to help him look for an apartment in DC the next day.

Chapter 2
The List Gets Longer

As the celebration began to quiet down Deacon told Kevin he had someone who wanted to meet him. It was the Naval Academy Commandant, Captain James Pierce. A reluctant Kevin, always wishing to live beneath the radar, followed Deacon into the polished wood adorned office with historical memorabilia that would have made any historical museum envious.

The Commandant beckoned the two in and offered them seats in a comfortable, yet orderly seating area. After asking if he could get them anything, they both declined, the Colonel addressed his orderly... "That will be all." He now turned his full attention to his guests.

"Mr. Flaherty, or should I say Lieutenant, would it be all right for purposes of our discussion today if I address you as Kevin? You may call me Jim."

Kevin nodded.

"Now the young Ensign has told me of the difference you've made in his life."

Kevin responded, "It has been an honor and a privilege to be of help Deacon."

Jim seeming to choose his words carefully, "And a Presidential referral, those do not come easily. Can you share how you were able to obtain it?"

Kevin, sensing an interrogation of sorts only offered, "I'm not a liberty to say."

The comments were a surprise to Deacon, he was never told or thought to ask where his referral had emanated from. He was even more impressed with Kevin than previously...which was hard to do.

Jim now persisted in his questioning, "And you knew Deacon's father?"

Kevin was growing more impatient with the direction the conversation was taking, responded succinctly, "Briefly."

Jim retorted, "You're a man of view words."

Kevin trying to remain courteous, but clearly rankled by direction being taken, "I try to be, especially when I do not understand the purpose of the questions."

Jim in a much more upbeat tone. "I can assure you the reason for my questions are in an incredibly positive light, but require a couple more inquiries, if you don't mind?"

Kevin less sharply, "Very well, please continue."

Jim now appeared to cross the line, "And you kept a list?"

Kevin now bristled, "This is a very private matter that I do not feel comfortable discussing with...pardon me Sir, acquaintances."

Jim apologetically, "I completely understand, but I believe I have some news specific to the aforenoted list that you will find fascinating."

Kevin now exasperated, "Go on."

Jim trying to get to the point more quickly, "And your list included 29 names."

Kevin simply nodded.

"I submit to you your list is wrong."

Kevin considered walking out of the office, but decided to stay in respect to Deacon offered, "The list painstakingly kept by me and no one else had access to it. I can assure you it is 100 percent accurate."

Jim leaned forward with elbows on his knees and looked directly into Kevins eyes, "I beg your pardon, its missing a name."

Kevin joined the deep stare into Jims eyes, "And who might that be?"

Jim said flatly, "Me."

Chapter 3
What Does It All Mean?

Both Kevin and Deacon were flabbergasted by the Commandant's statement. How could it be and how would Jim know it.

Jim seeing the perplexed look on his guests faces began to explain, "On your last recovery mission you were severely wounded and left for dead by the pilot of the copter. The other men of that crew were severely distraught on his decision. They wanted to retrieve your body, dead or alive, but the pilot had acted too quickly. Upon his return to base, he was assaulted by a Lieutenant Drake, a friend of yours and your regular pilot."

All of this rang true, but how did Jim know all the details? Jim continued, "You were pronounced KIA, awarded the medal of honor posthumously, provided a memorial service in Gainesville, Florida," Jim paused for a long moment and proceeded with "...I even met your parents."

This final comment hit Kevin the hardest, how, and why had Jim met his parents? Then it hit him...he was the 30th man. He uttered, "You were...?"

Jim without missing a beat jumped in, "Before you were hit you had delivered a pilot back to the chopper. As I turned to help you in you were hit twice, and before we could retrieve you the pilot pulled up and away."

Kevin was slumped over in his chair. He had not revisited that scene for a very long time, and the vivid nature of Jim's story telling hit him hard. Deacon had heard of it before, but never in such detail.

Chapter 4
Gratitude is a Funny Word

After allowing Kevin to absorb the entire story Jim spoke clearly and decidedly, "I owe you a debt of gratitude I can never fully repay."

The words seem to startle Kevin. He had never received this type of "thank you" from one of his pilots, and certainly not in the way it had been delivered.

Kevin looked up and in a surprising gesture asked, "You met my parents?"

Jim responded. "Yes, of course. I made a point of it. They were pretty broken up about it. How are they?"

Kevin in not wanting to get into the details commented, "They're fine, better than ever." Even Deacon nodded enthusiastically. They were like his Grand godparents.

All three of them pondered the significance of this recent discovery. Of course, there were small world comparisons to sift though, and Kevin always liked to hear the stories of the men he'd saved...had their lives made a difference for others? It was clear the rescue of Jim, while sending Kevin's life into a tumultuous period, had 'made a difference' for many others and for that he was grateful.

In beginning to think of what this wonderful coincidence meant, Jim was the first to suggest something to the group, "Kevin, I'd like to have you accept a visiting lecturer role in the Academy. You can visit us once a semester and talk about whatever you feel is relevant to our midshipmen. I would like to suggest the first topic be on Perseverance."

All expenses would be covered by the Academy, a consulting fee and honorarium to the Foundation. Kevin accepted the offer with, "It would be an honor."

While Kevin reflected on the day's developments, he sensed something else out there waiting for him, he just wished he knew what.

Chapter 5
Always Rely on Your Training First (and Last)

As Kevin found his way back to Les, she was his North Star, always there to guide him back to what truly mattered most, and he needed that guidance here...and he needed it here more than he knew.

After retelling the Commandant's story back to Les, including the role being offered to Kevin within the Academy, she was delighted. In her mind it was just another person owing their life to her heroic husband. She knew he could not see it that way, he never saw his actions in that light...just doing his job.

Secondly, the assignment in the Academy sounded great. An honor he deserved, and a chance to regain a focus, more meaning in his life. It was hard to imagine Kevin in this way, but besides the Foundation and his mentoring Deacon he did not have much else going on. Les blamed this partially on herself, her insistence on his remaining "retired" was partly to blame for his lack of motivation. She had even noticed a few extra pounds he was carrying, and while she found him just as handsome as the day she fell in love with him, like any good wife she worried about his health.

Finally, it was another financial windfall of sorts for the Foundation, and with its restructuring it could use all the additional funds it could find. After Kevin's request four years ago for the President to recognize Sam Grant's heroism and devotion to the service of his country, a request that had wonderfully caught Les off-guard, she had become the face of this portion of the Foundation, and the more money raised, the better work that could be done. She saw all of this as positive.

Deacon on the other hand was for lack of a better word...amazed! He knew his godfather had done some good things, maybe some remarkable things and quite possibly some heroic things, such as his attempt to save his father, but the description and what transpired in the Commandant's office took it to another level. He remarked, "So you were a real hero or something in your day?"

Kevin's reaction internally was 'or something' and 'in your day' hit him harder than expected. In a little over four years had he gone from what he had once been to this... 'it was better to be a has been than a never was'...right? Besides, he loved his new life. No adrenaline rushes, people trying to kill him, saving the damsel (Les) in distress...was this what people called a 'mid-life crises?'

Les saw the look on his face, "What's wrong?"

Kevin in a distracted tone, "Nothing (meaning everything), nothing at all." Still, what were the motives of this 30th man?

Chapter 6
Always Trust Your Instincts, You Can Apologize Later

The last time Kevin, then Jake, had truly trusted his instincts was when he suggested Roosevelt Lincoln was "dirty." It not only helped he and Les make it out of their situation alive, identify how the murder of Sam Grant was orchestrated and eventually led to a severe damaging of a major drug cartel, with the Patron still acting as an asset for law enforcement. Yes, his "instincts" in that case were right on.

This time it seemed improbable that the head of one of the Country's most elite and honorable institutions would be impossible to predict or believe, there were other examples of corruption at prestigious institutions or by individuals who seemed to have been beyond approach.

Kevin decided he would presume the best of intentions were meant by Jim but remain vigilant. As once was referenced in a nuclear proliferation treaty reification process...trust and verify. He made one inquire on the topic to his source within the agency, who was surprised to hear from him after the four plus year's hiatus. They were aware of the Commandant and had no direct concerns on his dossier, but on a personal level there was something he could not put his finger on.

Kevin's antenna remained up.

Chapter 7
Reflections

It had always been important to Kevin that the individuals he and his team rescued were good people, that they were or became members of the community that contributed, raised families, and provided goodwill towards their fellow man. Of course, there is no true way of tracking or determining the results of this goal, it was simply more aspirational, and Kevin and Daf had pondered it after the fact and over a few beers while serving.

During war and particularly among those who saw combat there was a sort of 'gallows' humor. In order to convince oneself into jumping out of a helicopter, while the enemy was shooting at you, to save an individual you had never met required courage, but also an ability to absorb the absurdity of the entire process. Sarcasm was a tool to reconcile all of it.

Kevin pondered all the intricacies in the journey that had taken him to this point. He was becoming better at compartmentalizing his memories, and only opening in most case the files he needed, when needed. After the fateful meeting with the Commandant of the Naval Academy it had reopened some old wounds, primarily why he was on that mission at all.

The morning in question was to be his last 'in country.' He had served his time, was being sent home finally with a few scrapes, and felt massive amounts of guilt for the Marines that would take his place in the copter, as well as those pilots who might not be rescued by him.

The definition of guilt reads; noun...the fact of having committed a specified or implied offense or crime "it is the duty of the prosecution to prove the prisoner's guilt," verb...make (someone) feel guilty, especially in order to induce them to do something." "Celeste had been guilted into going to her parents."

In going through his own version of Maslow's Hierarchy of Needs he realized the guilt he carried was his own, no one else had installed it for him, and more importantly it is why he had jumped on that last helicopter.

Chapter 8
A New Form of Adrenaline

Kevin's first lecture at the Academy was magical. As requested, he had built it around the topic Perseverance, and while he had hoped to inspire the 'middies' (informal for midshipmen), it was really he who had come away inspired.

The Q&A portion of the lecture was perhaps the most inspiring. The questions raised were thoughtful, articulate, and challenging. He ended his talk with a quote that had been passed down from his grandmother, "You can have it all, you just cannot have it all at the same time." This brought a modest ovation from the attendees, and Kevin thought to himself he was living proof of this quote.

The Commandant (Jim) came over to congratulate him and ask if he could buy him a beer. Kevin's flight was not until the next morning, so he graciously accepted, and besides he was in a celebratory mood. Jim suggested an Irish pub within walking distance, the Castlebay Irish Pub.

Kevin called Les on his way over. She was thrilled to hear how well it had gone and was sorry she missed it. She promised to be there next time. As they hung up, she could not resist saying "Sleep well, I love you!" She knew Kevin was still prone to nightmares that could be triggered by several sources, including being in a bar with a bunch of alpha males from a military academy. She had just created her own worries and again remembered her dad's saying, "Don't borrow trouble."

Chapter 9
The Good, the Bad and the Treacherous

Kevin arrived first at the pub. It was a weeknight, and he easily found a quiet booth tucked away from the crowd. He ordered a Guiness and began to wait for his guest to appear.

After his wonderful experience in Dublin at the Brazen and other traditional pubs he found the US versions satisfactory, but in most cases lacking a key ingredient, Seamus. There were other bartenders who poured the same and were as efficient in their job, but the intellect, humanity and genuine nature of his friend.

He looked up and saw Jim approaching the booth with another individual in tow. Jim introduced the man as Dwight Pierson and described him as another visiting lecturer who spoke on Political Science to the "middies." This surprised Kevin, he came from an era in which most military leaders were apolitical, at least until they retired, the most notable being George Washington, Ulysses S. Grant and Dwight Eisenhower.

As the other drink arrived Kevin asked Dwight if he was a politician himself and he answered in the negative, made a joke about his background not able to manage the scrutiny and went on to describe his role. All Kevin heard was "lobbyist."

As the three became a bit more comfortable Jim asked, "So tell me again, how you know the President?" This repeating a question or asking a question, you already knew the answer to...much like Rosie had done, set off a warning within Kevin's psyche. He repeated his original answer, "No, I said I was not at liberty to say."

The other two men pondered the answer while nodding their heads. Finally, Dwight followed up with, "And where did you have the opportunity to meet the President?"

Kevin was in no mood to play 20 Questions with these two men, especially one who is the head of a military academy who many think consider the finest in the nation, if not the world, and answered in his most direct manner while looking at Jim, "I expect you to understand what is meant when one officer says to another 'I am not at liberty to say'. Now, we can change the subject, or I will head back to my hotel."

Dwight reacted first, "Hey, there's no reason to get so hot and bothered by the question, we're just trying to gather some information on the current President on behalf of an organization we support, it's not that big of a deal. We're all just patriots trying to do what's best for the country we love."

Kevin noticed two clues on what he was dealing with in the pub, first, the look Jim gave Dwight when he mentioned "organization," and secondly the use of the phrase "patriots." It had been his experience that many "organizations" using this phrase were more subversive in their dealings. He decided to call their bluff in the questions being asked, and looking directly at Jim asked, "Can you share the name of this organization?"

Jim was clearly taken aback on his question and stammered, "Well, I guess we're not at liberty to say either."

At this point Dwight, not knowing to shut up added, "But we're confident that a man with your credentials would be supportive to our efforts." Again, Jim shot an even harder look towards Dwight, with the intention of shutting down the conversation and moving in a separate direction.

Unfortunately, Kevin moved first with a follow-up of his own with, "And just what are my credentials and what are the intentions of your organization?"

Jim had no choice but to shut things down quickly and dramatically due to Dwight's willingness to show their cards too quickly, "I think we need to change the subject here, there's no point in discussing these issues any further."

Kevin now reluctant to leave the subject and gesturing toward Dwight persisted with, "The man referenced my credentials and before we leave the topic and for reasons of clarity, I'd like hear what you think they are?"

Jim in an even more nervous tone interjected, "Just that you're an American hero, that's all."

To drive home his point Kevin spoke to both men, "I've never been comfortable with that phrase and refuse to wear it as my title. I have known a number of men and women who have stepped up on behalf of friends, family, and country to do the right thing, and a few who have paid the ultimate price for their actions. I do not belong in their company...and as far as your undisclosed intentions are concerned, I've taken to oaths in my life, one was to my wife and the other was to defend the Constitution, as I know Jim has as well."

Dwight could not help himself and blurted out, "And to follow orders!"

Kevin in moving his gaze from Jim to Dwight repeated, "Orders, what are you talking about?"

Before letting Dwight do any further damage, Jim motioned to Dwight and said, "Please find our server and settle up the tab. I'll meet you out front."

As soon as Dwight left them, he turned back towards Kevin, "I am sorry, that didn't go as well as I had hoped."

Kevin not leaving Jim's gaze added, "What had you hoped for?"

Jim answered, "Just an exchange of ideas on what's best for our country. We should leave it at that for now."

Kevin responded, "Very well, thanks for the beer." He got up slowly and looked once more and said in passing, "I have a good topic for the next lecture.

Jim in a curious manner asked, "What is that?"

Kevin in his most serious tone, "What an oath means."

Footnote: I do solemnly swear that I will support and defend the Constitution of the United States against all enemies, foreign and domestic; that I will bear true faith and allegiance to the same; and that I will obey the orders of the President of the United States and the orders of the officers appointed ...

Chapter 10
A Fine Mess

As soon as Jim walked out of the pub Dwight began to comment on the meeting, "I thought he was on our side? That was awful. I cannot believe his responses to our questions."

Jim in a hushed voice, "Please be quiet, we need to move to a more secure spot before we debrief on this 'train wreck'." The use of the phrase meaning to alert Dwight on just how poorly he had performed.

After walking a few blocks, they found a park bench and sat down together. Jim began with, "You are reckless! You not only failed in our recruitment efforts of Mr. Flaherty, but you have also filled his head with questions about what we are up to. You have taken one golden opportunity and created two problems. My recommendation to the Council will be to remove you from all other recruitment efforts, and I am thinking their actions might be even more severe."

Evin more severe...Dwight could not believe what he was a loyal and hardworking member of the cause. Surely his past efforts and accomplishments would help support the case being made by his superior within the organization and attempted to build a case with Jim.

Jim cutting to the chaste, "All of that is well and good, but we cannot afford reckless behavior, especially when we're dealing with the likes of Mr. Flaherty...you loaded his gun, now we just need to hope he doesn't act on his suspicions."

Chapter 11
There is No Choice

K evin tried to justify in his own mid the events of the night before, but there were too many concerns to dismiss what he felt was a) an interrogation of him, and b) a disclosure of what seems to be a nefarious organization.

Kevin was not naïve; he knew there were many groups and divisive feeling in the country today, and in a democracy, everyone is entitled to their own opinions...even in the military. However, the thought of the Commandant of one of the elite institutions in the country involved in something like it should be alarming.

He desperately wanted to keep Deacon out of the situation he was facing. If he were wrong it could be harmful to his career, and if he was right in his concerns Deacon could be used as a pawn or worse. He decided to begin with the passive approach.

Deacon picked up the phone on the 2nd ring and greeted Kevin with, "Hello Cap!" He had begun calling begun calling Kevin 'Captain America' after hearing of his exploits from Jim after his graduation. Kevin didn't appreciate the full moniker but didn't mind Cap... after all he had gone by several names in his undercover days. Deacon continued, "How was your lecture professor?"

Kevin was quick to share the positive elements of the night before, and it was a natural lead into the real purpose of his call. When Kevin asked if there were any fringe elements within the Naval Academy he was greeted with an affirmative response, and a reference to all college campuses having differing opinions on political leadership. He was also quick to point out that they tried to stay under the radar for obvious reasons but felt there were no clandestine activities.

Kevin gently asked if he was aware of the faculty 'stirring the pot'? Deacon initially denied this being the case but then recalled a guest lecturer who promoted some more extreme actions, and like many extreme or fringe elements tried to paint the Founding Fathers as their own brand of 'terrorists'.

Kevin asked if he remembered the name of the guest lecturer and Deacon replied, "It was Dwight something..."

Chapter 12
Connecting the Dots

K evin thought to himself, 'why can't I stay retired?' It was true, no matter how he tried, it seemed his 'normal' life would always escape him. Perhaps he was destined to struggle with and pursue complex and possibly dangerous activities.

He decided to get his facts in order and assess if what conclusions were being drawn made sense:

- Was there a chance he 'jumping the gun' on developing the scenario of Jim and Dwight representing some sinister extremist organization.
- What did he really know about Jim? Other than the fact he qualified as Kevin's 30th man and was now the commandant of the Naval Academy not much. There was a huge gap in his resume and things like family history, that could tell him some key clues.
- And then there was Dwight, what could be possibly his role in this case. It seemed to Kevin he was not 'up to the task' of fronting an organization in the same way Jim was...how could he fit.

Kevin needed to make a few phone calls, but before he could his phone buzzed.

Chapter 13
First Things First

He expected it to be Les but the voice on the other end was clearly not feminine, "Kevin, this is Jim. Again, I am sorry about how the evening ended last night, and wanted to know if you could join me for breakfast in the Officer's Mess this morning?"

Kevin in keeping his cards to himself responded, "Yes, I would have liked to, but I have a plane to catch this morning."

Jim said, "We'll do it another time." He paused and then interjected, "You must have thought Dwight and I acted like a couple buffoons last night with all this talk about mysterious organizations and all."

Kevin thought Jim was trying to make light of a situation that carried no pretense of lightness and responded, "Well no that's not the word I was thinking of to describe our conversation."

Jim laughed his comment off and proceeded with, "You see Dwight is an author and we're co-writing a novel about a mysterious organization within the Naval Academy. Kind of a political thriller, and we are thinking about writing you, or should I say someone like you as a character in the book."

Kevin absorbed what had been said and followed with, "So, this is a work of fiction?"

Jim eagerly, "Absolutely, but we need it to have some border line facts to make it seem real."

It was now Kevin's turn to interrogate, "Does your CO know you are working on this novel?"

Jim with a curt response, "Well no, and I'd appreciate you not sharing this with anyone else."

More secrets thought Kevin, "Does this explain why Dwight was brought in as a speaker at the Academy?"

He could hear the dismay in Jim's voice, "Yes, just more background for the book."

Jim thought to himself, 'how would Kevin know about that and then remembered his godson, Deacon... "Yes, and I'd keep that to yourself as well."

Kevin replied tersely, "That's a lot of secrets we're accumulating, and while I'm pretty good with secrets, I've been told I'm a bad liar."

Jim now off his script, "What is that supposed to mean?"

Kevin said in a straightforward manner, "If someone asks me a question, I am usually going to tell them the truth."

Jim paused and then responded, "I'll keep that in mind for future conversations. Have a nice day."

Chapter 14
Get to Work

A s soon as he hung up the phone with Jim, he called his long-lost contact within the agency. After updating him on his efforts to remain 'retired' he asked the question on Jim's background.

Surprisingly, he was told that Jim's background on a personal level was beyond reproach from a war hero to continued service to the country had led him to his current role as Commandant to the Naval Academy. There were many who suggested his future would extend beyond the Academy and could reach as high as a senior cabinet level appointment. It was not believed he had political interests beyond that level.

An area of concern revolved around his current marriage. He had divorced his high school sweetheart with their three sons and quickly remarried his second wife. Maya, although suggesting to some in DC social circles as being Latina and describing her exotic appearance as being due to a blending of Spanish/Moorish descendance, was full-blooded Arabic, with friends and family in some lofty, yet troubling positions of power with links to even some shadier connections.

Her background was either dismissed or unvetted to Jim's reputation and rank within the Navy. This oversight was being updated within the national security community, and on another level, they were collaborating with the FBI on related investigations.

Kevin was pleased to know his instincts into these matters were still sound but wished in another way they were not.

Chapter 15
Trust Is Earned

K evin was seeing the picture more clearly, but there were still some elements that needed to be flushed out more fully. He would need additional resources as well; he suspected this organization was bigger than he suspected.

He dialed a number he had not used for approximately four years and felt bad for not staying in touch with the person who answered the call, "Special Agent Walker."

Kevin started with, "Glad you haven't retired yet."

To which Walker replied, "Are you kidding, don't you know crime, including treason and drug smuggling are growth industries."

Kevin nodding his head asked, "You gotta minute?"

After sharing the specifics along with updates on Les and Deacon Kevin asked, "Do you think I'm onto something or am I just chasing windmills?"

Walker responded with, "I know you're on to something" and proceeded to fill in the blanks from the FBI Task Force he was heading up.

He concluded his portion of the debrief with, "We presumed someone within the military was involved, but hadn't figured out the source yet. I think you might have done us a major favor in outing the Commandant. Our next step will be to work on his role and who else might be involved."

Kevin was quiet for what seemed like an eternity but was lost in thought. He broke the silence with, "I think I can help. Can you get me a wire (industry speak for a high-tech recording device) and a firearm?"

Walker said he would have them both within the hour.

Then Kevin asked one final question, "Do you know what their next steps will be?"

Walker breathed in and out slowly and proceeded with, "To disrupt our government...by assassinating the President and perhaps other key leaders."

Kevin replied, "Roger that."

Chapter 16
I Hope You Can Understand

K evin was not looking forward to the next call, and when Les answered she immediately sensed something, "What's wrong?" Kevin wished he could answer with nothing and move onto a more regular conversation, but as he had once assured her with "I can tell you anything' he needed to come clean.

He started with, "I've stumbled into something that I need to work through...it's regarding national security and it should only take a few days at most."

Les had learned to hate that term 'national security', as it always put loved ones in harm's way. She absorbed what had been said and answered with, "Will you be in danger?" She knew Kevin could never disclose more details.

Kevin said in a solemn tone, "I don't think so." Again, Les knew in operative code speak this meant 'probably some'. While she desperately wanted to talk him out of it, she knew it would be a waste of her time and pulling on his 'heart strings' could easily distract him.

She opted for a sterile, "We'll expect you in a few days. I love you."

All Kevin could muster was, "I do too."

He wrestled with getting involved and knew it was a task that could not be done without 100% commitment on his part. He was in or out...and knew what needed to be done.

Chapter 17
It Cannot Be This Easy

Kevin received a text from Walker with a phone number and dialed it immediately sensing it would be a much easier call to make. The phone at the other end was answered quickly with a voice saying, "Hello this is Dwight."

Even though it was unrehearsed Kevin knew exactly what to say, "Dwight, this is Kevin Flaherty. I'm sorry about how things went down last night and thinking I have some information that might be of help regarding my relationship with the President."

Dwight could barely process the words and all he could think was 'this is how I get back in good graces with Jim.' He tried to suppress the giddiness in his voice and said simply, "That's good to hear...maybe we should plan on meeting."

Kevin in the affirmative, "That would be great, do you know where Horn Point Park is? Let's plan on meeting around 1900 hours after the tourists have left. Will Jim be joining us?"

Dwight responded quickly, "Yes I do, and no that will not be necessary. See you at 1900 hours." Having never been in the military, he still liked to act as though he had.

Kevin thought, this is perfect the trap was set.

Chapter 18
Casing the Joint

As he had done many times before, with one memory from Barcelona, he needed to know his terrain. The discipline of his days as an operative for the agency fused with his new life, his better life.

During his best days as an effective agent these types of pleasant memories would not have interfered with his thinking or his actions.

However, Barcelona creeped back into his consciousness, and as pleasant as the jade dress was in his mind...especially when Les slipped out of it, he needed to flush it from his mind. These are the distractions that got operatives killed.

He took the time to call Deacon. He assured him the reason for his staying over was to do some sightseeing and meet a friend for dinner. Deacon told him to have fun.

Then Kevin made a huge mistake!

Chapter 19
Arlington National Cemetery/
The Wall (aka the Vietnam War Memorial)

L ike most veteran's Kevin appreciated the solemn ground of
places like Arlington Cemetery and other memorials to
brothers in arms, even those in foreign lands like the Valley
of the Fallen outside Madrid that he shared with Les during their
courtship.

Most people do not know that Arlington Cemetery is built on 637
acres (about the area of Central Park in New York City) that once
belonged to the family of Robert E. Lee. It is the final resting place
for many American soldiers, sailors, and Marines, as well as ex-
Presidents like John F. Kennedy who had been a WWII hero himself
on PT 109.

Kevin was there to see one grave; it was the second time he had
visited the gravesite of on Donald "Daffy" Drake. As he saluted his
old friend and personal hero he asked for guidance during the next
few hours. He had a lot to live for thanks to 'Daf'. While it was an
emotional moment it would not come close to his next stop.

The Vietnam war Memorial while being a stark reminder of a very
unpopular war, was a cathartic experience for veterans and family
members who had lost loved ones. The personalization of names
being embedded in the marble edifice. For Kevin this all rang true
with the major difference being...his name was carved into the wall
as well.

This hit him like a 'ton of bricks' and he barely made it back to
his hotel room be before breaking into sobs and reliving some of the
nightmares while wide awake. This was no way to prepare for an
important assignment.

Chapter 20
Showtime

By 1700 hours he was feeling a bit better and jumped into a cold shower to regain all his senses. He was not too worried about handling Dwight. There was nothing to suggest he was capable of inflicting anything on an adversary, but you never could take these things for granted.

When he arrived at the agreed upon bench they exchanged minimal pleasantries, and Dwight went right to work, "What can you tell me about the President and how can you help us?"

Kevin responded with, "I can tell you practically anything you need to know. I was the lead on his security detail for many years." This is a complete fabrication but did not think Dwight had anyway of disputing it. It served its purpose with Dwight leaning in more closely to hear everything. Kevin followed up with, "I want to do more than just provide data, I want to be involved in the organization...maybe even act as a 'triggerman' on future hits."

This was going even better than Dwight had hoped for, it would surely get him back in Jim's good graces. Just then the two men heard a rustling of leaves and turned to see Jim step out of the bushes with a handgun equipped with a silencer. He looked at Dwight first a in the harshest of tones barked, "You imbecile, you just couldn't leave well enough alone."

Both men had their hands raised and Jim spoke now looking at Kevin and said, "Trying to be the hero again? Not receiving enough accolades lately."

Kevin shook his head from side to side and spoke, "Nope, just following my oath, you remember it. Or do you?"

Another person joined the group following Kevin's remarks, it was Deacon with a handgun pointed squarely at the Commandant's back. It was his turn to issue orders, "Sir, please drop your weapon."

The Commandant in his most authoritative voice shouted, "Stand down Lieutenant."

Deacon responded with, "I cannot carry out that order, sir."

The Commandant replied with, "My mission is accomplished" and discharged his silenced weapon.

The bullet entered Kevin near where one of the previous shots had hit him. As he fell backwards, he heard another weapon discharge, this time without a silencer, and hoped Deacon had taken the Commandant out. Moments later Deacon cradled Kevin in his arms and said, "Dad, I mean Kevin, are you OK?"

The mistaken reference brought a smile to his face, it was a role he would never get to play.

A helicopter hovered over the scene and illuminated most of the park. The bushes rustled again, and this time Walker made his entrance with several other FBI agents. He quickly surveyed the scene and gestured for his men to take Dwight into custody. Walking towards Kevin and Deacon he calmly got on his radio and announced, "Officer down need medical support immediately!"

He walked over to Kevin and Deacon and uttered, "This wasn't part of the plan."

Kevin looked up at Deacon and whispered, "How did you know?"

Deacon replied, "Les asked me to keep an eye on you."

Kevin again smiled and whispered again, "She did, did she. Well, tell her" ...he drifted off into unconsciousness.

Walker seeing his friends' eyes close told his men, "Bring him to my car and put him in the backseat, we have no time to waste."

Deacon fighting back tears now helped them carry the man who had turned his life around. From the hospital he called Les and told her he was being taken into surgery; she was with his parents. All they could think of was, not again.

Chapter 21
An Understanding

There is fulfilling one's destiny and then there is going beyond the call of duty. In this case Kevin had far exceeded his call of duty and on two occasions had nearly paid the ultimate price on numerous occasions. Why is an individual wired in this way and seemed to keep running into these types of situations. If you were to ask Kevin he would probably say, "Just lucky I guess."

However, vigilance is a trait not all are born with or acquire in their lifetime. Many people would have dismissed Jim's persistent questioning as mere curiosity about the leader of the free world. Kevin saw it as something more and it was those instincts that proved invaluable for field work. An internal analyst could not have these instincts or even if they did acquire them, it could not be complete without being able to look into the perpetrators eyes or as they are often called the 'windows to the soul'

As Kevin came out of the fog of surgery, he sensed two feelings: 1) the pulsating pain in his upper right chest, and 2) the warmth of another's hand holding his hand. His eyes slowly opened to a vision of an angel standing over him. Of course, it was not an angel, but certainly it was the next best thing.

Les leaned over and gently kissed him on the cheek. He was not ready for her standard firm yet soft lips pressing against his at this point in his recovery but would be soon. She looked him squarely in the eye and whispered in his ear, "If you ever try another stunt like that, I'll kill you!" There was not a doubt in his mind.

She then asked, "Tell me what?" He looked at her quizzically. "Deacon said you started to say something before you passed out."

He smiled and said, "I do too!"

Footnotes: The papers reported an altercation in the park yesterday evening. Details would be released soon, but it was believed senior naval officers had been involved in a sting-type operation.

Dwight cooperated fully and the next morning subpoenas and arrest warrants were delivered to a dozen military and political leaders. Their charges included treason and intent to overthrow the government through violent insurrection.

Kevin was only acknowledged as a former law enforcement officer who was seriously wounded, no name given.

Deacon served his country as a systems engineer assigned to the Pentagon for his required term. He now runs a start-up software company in Encinitas, California. He is married with two young boys, Miles and Jake.

Les made Kevin promise to no longer pay attention to his instincts.

About the Author

Brian is a retired insurance/consulting executive who grew up in Pasadena, CA and now lives in Irvine, CA. Brian lives with Parkinson's Disease and spends much of his time raising awareness of the disease and funds for the Michael J. Fox Foundation (MJFF) through the OC Ride for Parkinson's Disease. He is dedicating 10% of the proceeds of this book to the MJFF."